This field guide belongs to

This book provides insight and information about the life, habits, and habitats of the denizens of the Invisible World. The authors wish to confirm that in opening this book, you agree that you will be responsible for the knowledge contained within and will use it wisely.

—T. D. & H. B.

"I believe when I am in the mood that all nature is full of people whom we cannot see, and that some of these are ugly or grotesque, and some wicked or foolish, but very many beautiful beyond any one we have ever seen, and that these are not far away. . . . the simple of all times and the wise men of ancient times have seen them and even spoken to them."

— W. B. Yeats, *The Celtic Twilight*

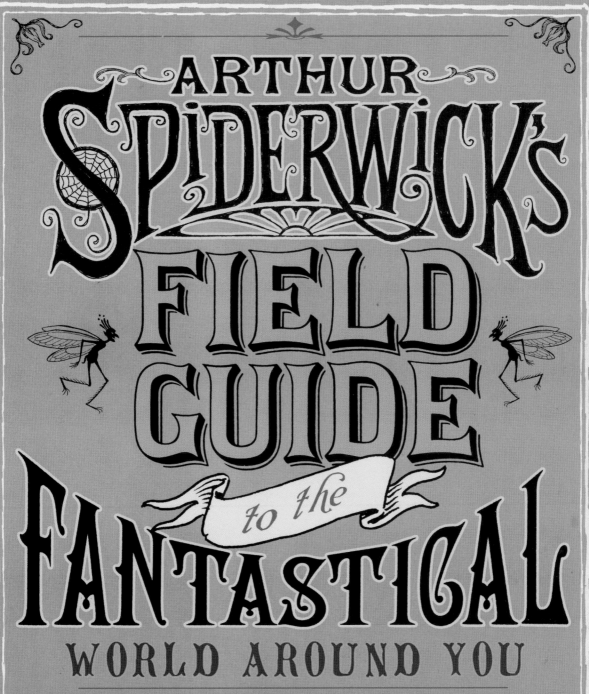

ARTHUR SPIDERWICK'S FIELD GUIDE *to the* FANTASTICAL WORLD AROUND YOU

ACCURATELY RESTORED and DESCRIBED BY

TONY DiTERLIZZI and HOLLY BLACK

SIMON & SCHUSTER BOOKS FOR YOUNG READERS
NEW YORK   LONDON   TORONTO   SYDNEY

TABLE OF CONTENTS

AROUND THE HOUSE AND YARD

IN FIELDS AND FORESTS

In Lakes, Streams, and the Sea

In the Hills and Mountains

In the Sky

Outside at Night

August 22nd, 1935

Smithsonian Institute
Washington, District of Columbia

Dear Sir or Madam,

I began the book you see before you many years ago, after my brother was killed and devoured, before my very eyes, by a troll. I determined that none of us would be safe so long as we continued to ignore the possibility that there were fantastical creatures among us, hidden through mimicry and magic. I vowed that I would devote my adult life to revealing this Invisible World.

It is my hope that you will consider my book—the fruits of many years of study—for publication. You have put out many fine scientific texts and I know that if my guide was printed through your offices, I could finally achieve a wide enough readership to really succeed in informing people of my findings.

I have undertaken an illustrated study of those beings I was able to observe in nature. In doing so, I have noticed that some of my observations conflict with the descriptions I have found in folklore and with renderings from antique bestiaries. I have identified several reasons why this might be so. I have found that in several old woodcuts the creatures are depicted with more human attributes than I was able to observe. This anthropomorphizing may be a stylistic choice on the part of the artist or a way to exploit the sensational nature of the subject matter.

I have also noticed that many of the creatures are recorded as being larger and more powerful than my observations indicate. I believe this is simply a result of what I call "the big fish effect," whereby as the stories of a creature spread out from their source, the creature's attributes were embellished for effect.

Further, although I have tried to classify the beings I've observed, I am in no way confident that my classifications will stand up to rigorous analysis. The shifting nature and form of the fey folk seem to defy categorization. It is my singular hope that the work I have done will help prove the existence of the Invisible World and draw the interest of more naturalists. Only through exhaustive study will we be able to penetrate its many mysteries.

I eagerly await your response.

Arthur Spiderwick

Foreword

What is real? This is a question I've often asked myself, and although the answer seems simple enough, the more I think about it, the harder it is to figure out.

In looking through ancient bestiaries, I have found countless entries for animals most people would say couldn't possibly be real. Yet in some of those texts I have seen illustrations and highly detailed descriptions of creatures like cockatrices, unicorns, mermaids, and even faeries, all said to be based on eyewitness accounts. These stories stretch back hundreds and sometimes even thousands of years. This folklore feeds many famous fairy tales. But just because those ancient accounts are today mostly used for the delight of children, does that mean that no part of these accounts is now or ever has been real?

While on tour for the Spiderwick Chronicles, Holly and I met a little girl who shared that she had seen a living unicorn. Her mother didn't believe her. The little girl wanted us to validate what she had observed, and while her experience could have been imagined, she was convinced that it actually happened. Who are we to say it didn't? So what is real?

I am often asked if I've ever seen a faerie. As if not seeing a thing makes it less real. I can't see microbes, but they are everywhere, in the millions. They are just too small to see with the naked eye. And for hundreds of years people didn't even know they existed. That didn't mean they were not real. I've never seen many of the bizarre deep-sea fish that exist in the inky depths of the ocean, but I've observed models of them in museums with detailed notes similar to those in ancient bestiaries. How do I know that they're real? If we haven't seen faeries, perhaps it's because we don't have the right tools, or we haven't looked closely enough, or we've simply chosen not to acknowledge what we have seen or learned.

The more researchers and scientists explore the Earth's natural and ancient wonders, the more they discover. Who knows where these new discoveries will lead. The more folklore Holly and I read and compared with the fantastic observations of Arthur Spiderwick's, the more aware we became of what we didn't really know. And the more we wondered: WHAT IS REAL?

Arthur Spiderwick began the book you are holding more than one hundred years ago. Holly and I first learned of him and his studies through three of his surviving descendants, Jared, Simon, and Mallory Grace. They presented us with a book created by Arthur that was full of artwork and notes very similar to what you will see on the pages of this guide. Holly and I painstakingly organized and restored that work to create this volume.

Arthur Spiderwick's experiences are truly unique, and our hopes are that this work will not only add to the wonderment and research of fantastic folklore but also give readers a chance to ponder what is real.

Tony DiTerlizzi
Amherst, Massachusetts, 2005

The Invisible World

The first question that springs to mind when contemplating the existence of faeries is usually: *Where are they?* Doubters quickly follow with a second question: *Why can't I see them?* The answers are simultaneously simple and profound. The faerie world is all around you. In ancient forests. Beneath the still earth and rolling waves. Among the clouds and even under your own roof. But there is a catch. Faeries, as a rule, do not wish to be seen. Because of this, their world is commonly referred to as the *Invisible World*. And most simply explained, it's a world within our own, but where nothing is necessarily as it seems.

For starters, time passes differently among faeries. What might feel like a short dance among some toadstools could last for months, or even decades. And those hapless enough to travel into faerie hills may find that a hundred years have passed in moments.

Additionally, their need not to be seen makes spotting the denizens of the Invisible World a formidable task. To remain concealed, faeries employ *glamour*, a kind of magic, to disguise themselves. Goblins can appear like large toads with dried leaves for ears. Trolls might seem to be mossy boulders. Sprites may look like insects. Within the Invisible World, forms are fluid and changeable. And if they choose to, faeries can disappear completely.

Despite their illusive qualities, inhabitants of the Invisible World require respect. Solitary faeries—those that prefer not to live with their own kind—don't want their isolated existence interrupted and aim to control their interactions with humanity. Trooping faeries—those that live in large social groups—are offended by people trodding along their paths or snooping around the places of their revels. And while some faerie beasts are benevolent, many should be avoided at all costs. For this reason, a clear understanding of what the Invisible World is and how humans might interact with it is advantageous for any wanting to steer clear of wrathful fey. On the other hand, there are those who consider themselves to be adventurous and seek out faeries. If you are one of the latter, despite your curiosity, proceed with caution.

~ It must also be noted that the word "faerie" is loosely used here to describe any fantastical creature. Some of the beasts in this guide (like the manticore, sea serpent, and griffin) were thought to be monsters of myth, but they do employ similar methods of disguise as the "little folk."

The Sight

The ability to see into the Invisible World is simply called the *Sight*. If you are the seventh son of a seventh son, the seventh daughter of a seventh daughter, or if you were born with red hair, you may already have the Sight.

If you don't already have the Sight, a seeing stone—a rock that has had a hole bored through its center by some natural means, such as running water—can be employed. If you look through the stone's hole, you will have the Sight for as long as you are looking through it. Likewise, looking through any circle—even the circle of someone's arm as their hand rests on their hip—can allow the viewer to see into Faerie. But no makeshift circle is as effective as a true seeing stone.

Faerie ointment rubbed in the eyelids will also let you see faeries. Faeries put it on the eyes of their children soon after birth. This ointment is created from four-leaf clovers, although little more is known about it. A less potent unguent can be made from faerie bathwater, and some faerie enthusiasts leave basins of water outside for the purpose of attracting faeries to bathe therein.

It's important to note that the act of touching someone with the Sight will cause the person who is doing the touching to see into the Invisible World for as long as there is contact. The ability to "see" ends when the contact is terminated.

Faeries can sometimes be seen by those without the Sight at "between times" such as dawn and twilight, when it is not quite day and not quite night. Children and teenagers, due to their transitional growing state, are more likely to see faeries than adults. "Between places" are also good for spotting faeries—keeping one foot on land and the other in water works well, although any of these methods may draw unwanted attention from the fantastical world.

I found this seeing stone in Robinson Creek. This item has enabled me to see into the Invisible World and render the images you will find in these pages.

RENDERED ACTUAL SIZE

Equipment and Protection

Before one begins an expedition to observe the habits and habitats of fantastical creatures, there are several useful items one should collect.

A thermos with milk for appeasing and luring faeries. They like milk best lukewarm.

One twig each from an oak, an ash, and a thorn tree. Bind these together with red thread, and this will offer protection against faerie folk.

Shown here are:
AMERICAN MOUNTAIN ASH (*Sorbus americana*)
HONEY LOCUST (*Gleditsia tricanthos*)
SCARLET OAK (*Quercus coccinea*)

A magnifying glass comes in handy, especially when studying smaller creatures like sprites and salamanders.

A bag of salt can dispell some magical illusions, and many faeries cannot abide it.

Bring a journal (and pencils) to record all of your findings. You never know what you may come across.

It should be noted that the color red is protective, but faeries do not like the color and will shy away from it in the same manner that bees fly from smoke, making the faeries more difficult to find. The color green will, by contrast, draw faeries, but they may not be pleased to find a human wearing their color.

When hunting for nocturnal creatures such as banshees and will-o'-the-wisps, a flashlight is quite helpful.

A backpack or satchel is useful for carrying everything. Make sure it has an iron or steel clasp to keep pixies from stealing your inventory!

LIST OF PLATES

*All creatures rendered within are represented in
their truest form without the trickery of glamour.*

Color study of our estate looking west
July 9th, 1921

Around the House and Yard

From helpful brownies to troublesome boggarts, mysterious changelings to thieving pixies, fiery salamanders to baffling stray sod, the faeries that are closest to humans in proximity are not always the most friendly.

PLATE I

His cap is made of mouse leather.

This brownie lives within the walls of our house. His name is Thimbletack.

Thimbletack has beady black eyes and whiskers like a rodent.

His pail is a large thimble, and he cut a piece out of a dish sponge from the kitchen.

His shirt used to belong to a doll from my daughter's dollhouse.

A badminton shuttlecock, with a straight pin in it, serves as his feather duster.

His hands are very calloused.

One of my dress socks was used to make his pants.

A. Spiderwick

Custos domesticus
COMMON HOUSE BROWNIE
RENDERED ACTUAL SIZE

Brownies

FAMILY: HOMUNCULIDAE

These kindly and dependable creatures (also called *lobs*, *hobs*, or, if female, *silkies*) attach themselves to human households, where they help with chores and protect the well-being of people living on "their" land.

Fiercely loyal, *brownies* will defend a home and its surrounding estate from burglars and goblins. They live somewhere on the land they protect, perhaps in an abandoned barn, an unused closet, or within the walls. Despite their love of cleanliness, brownies are rather shabby in appearance, often going shoeless or wholly unclothed. Even so, they expect no payment other than scraps of food and a bowl of milk left out at night; in fact, further gifts are likely to induce adverse effects.

Shuffling sounds at night can be a sign of a brownie. The careful observer may be able to spy one at work if he or she can sneak up quietly enough. Even if not actually seen, the brownie may disappear in the middle of completing a task, leaving proof in the form of half-finished mopping or partially washed dishes.

~ In a house with a brownie you may find small, handmade brooms, dustpans, and other cleaning equipment.

~ Scattering sugar or flour on the floor is one way of obtaining footprints that might prove brownie activity. The problem with this method is that your brownie may simply clean up the mess.

~3~

This fellow's name was Dandersnuff.

If you are trying to attract a brownie, you would do well to leave porridge out as advertisement.

<u>*Recipe for porridge*</u>

1. Heat milk and then stir in flour until the mixture thickens.

2. After that, add sugar and a pat of butter on top.

3. Leave this out at night and your family brownie will be pleased.

He lived in the studio of a landscape painter and would clean his brushes at night.

Unusual organization of items is also common in houses with brownies. A brownie may alphabetize books by the middle initial of the authors' names or file records by the titles of favorite songs.

Industrious themselves, even the gentlest of brownies hates laziness in others. If taken advantage of, or otherwise ill-used, the brownie may become a boggart. (Compare to boggart, p. 6; leprechaun, p. 35; and knocker, p. 86.)

Champagne chairs constructed from discarded cork and wire bottle harnesses.

~ If you search carefully enough, you may be able to find a brownie's lair. This will always be in an unused part of the house and will contain spartan furnishings. The brownie may have constructed a bed for itself from a doll cradle or bundles of straw, or it may have even made a cobweb hammock.

Not all brownies looked like Thimbletack. This fellow, named Tam Turttedove, lived in a very old home in a nearby town.

As with many sightings I've researched, only the children of the household could see him.

Tam was a "mender." At night he would patch holes in clothing and even fix shoes. I wonder if the cobblers in the fairy tale "The Elves and the Shoemaker" were, in fact, brownies.

PLATE II

RENDERED ONE-HALF ACTUAL SIZE

Tam's pincushion
found under kitchen
floorboard

He has stitched leather knee pads
onto his trousers, made from a sock.

Custos domesticus
COMMON HOUSE BROWNIE
RENDERED ACTUAL SIZE

Boggarts
FAMILY: HOMUNCULIDAE

Abuse of a brownie, either through neglect of chores, failure to leave out food, or deliberate insult, will turn it into a *boggart*.

Also known as *bogans* or *bogies*, boggarts delight in tormenting those they once protected and will cause milk to sour, doors to slam, dogs to go lame, and other mischief.

Boggarts particularly like to steal food and to hide household items like keys and socks. More common than brownies, boggarts reside in many houses and workplaces. This may be the result of decades of improper treatment of brownies, which were once far more prevalent.

~6~

June 23rd, 1918

I wonder if the transformation from brownie to boggart is a physical one, or more a shift in mental state?

Can a boggart be transformed back into a brownie with an opposite action of kindness?

July 5th, 1918

I spoke with Thimbletack today about my theory of boggart-to-brownie transformation. He doubted its success.

Pair of scissors confiscated from the Riggenbach boggart. He was using them to snip the house cat's whiskers!

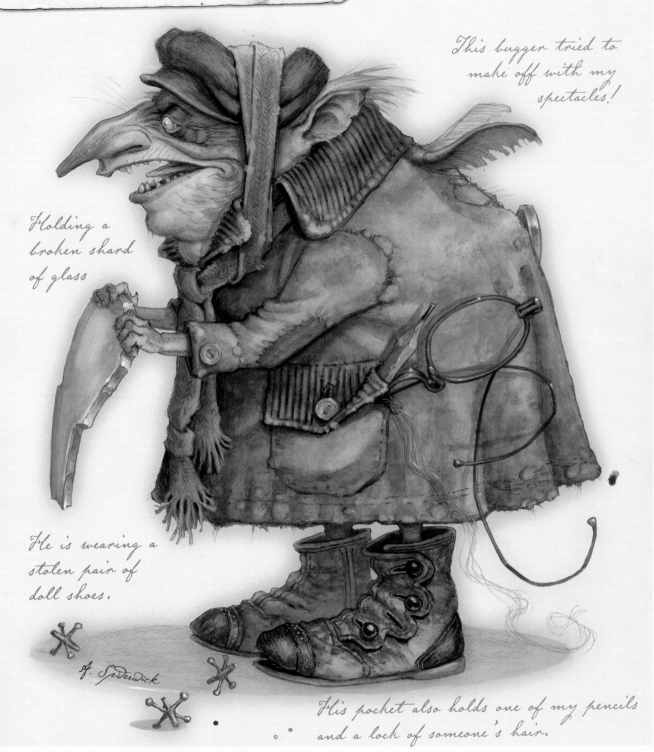

September 6th, 1909

I visited the Riggenbach estate today, as
its owners were convinced it was haunted.
However, it appears to be no more than
the handiwork of a particularly mischievous
boggart.

PLATE III

The Riggenbach boggart has
small, vestigial wings.

This bugger tried to
make off with my
spectacles!

Holding a
broken shard
of glass

He is wearing a
stolen pair of
doll shoes.

His pocket also holds one of my pencils
and a lock of someone's hair.

Custos domesticus

COMMON HOUSE BOGGART

RENDERED ACTUAL SIZE

PLATE IV

A large but shy boggart, named Lickspittle, that I discovered in a town nearby. His mischief seemed less malicious than the usual boggart fare. In fact, he reminded me strongly of a hobgoblin.

This rogue was stealing an infant's milk bottle each night and drinking it, leaving a hungry and screaming baby.

He had made his home in the chimney, and he left sooty footprints all over the floor each morning.

A. Spiderwick

Custos domesticus
COMMON HOUSE BOGGART
RENDERED ONE-HALF ACTUAL SIZE

As loyal as brownies, boggarts are almost impossible to get rid of. Many families have fled a house tormented by a boggart only to find the boggart fleeing with them.

Boggarts are sometimes confused with poltergeists because both terrorize households. And as both generally remain unseen, it can be hard to tell the difference. Listen carefully after something goes awry; if muffled laughter is heard, a boggart is the likely culprit. (Compare to brownie, p. 3, and hobgoblin, p. 85.)

October 14th, 1924

I've found no conclusive evidence of the existence of bugbears, or bugaboos.

My research has proven that these entries are completely fabricated, with the intent of spooking children into good behavior.

With all of the actual faerie species out and about, I truly feel that imagined creatures are hardly appropriate for discipline and only hinder the belief in true faeries.

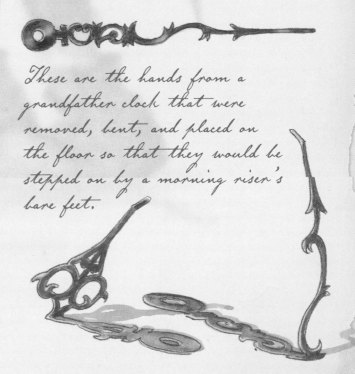

These are the hands from a grandfather clock that were removed, bent, and placed on the floor so that they would be stepped on by a morning riser's bare feet.

Changelings
FAMILY: CIRCULIFESTIDAE

Changelings are creatures from the Invisible World that have taken on the form of a human, usually a child, while that person is carried away to live among the faeries. Elves and pixies are most commonly the culprits, either leaving behind one of their own to grow up among mortals or leaving a piece of wood enchanted to look like the mortal that was stolen. Sometimes the changeling will fake its own death or mysteriously disappear in order to rejoin its own family (now one member larger with the addition of a human brother or sister).

There are various methods of protecting a child from being stolen: leaving open iron scissors where the child sleeps (dangerous and not recommended), placing a key on the child's blankets, turning the father's trousers inside-out and hanging them over the cradle, or stringing bundles of rowan and garlic along the sides of the infant's bed. Despite the abundance of methods, however, few are employed today.

Changelings often have distinct characteristics that set them apart from other children. They may have a tail, a hunched back, or a withered appearance, even if very young. They may also develop a grayish or greenish tone to their skin. A changeling

Changelings are often precocious for their age and will ask and answer sophisticated questions but will seem unfamiliar with common devices. Terrance was especially intrigued by my glasses.

This is Terrance Fink, a changeling boy raised by a family of farmers in upstate New York.

Terrance was probably swapped when the Finks' newborn was brought home from the hospital.

The Finks contacted me and I came out to investigate. My findings are as follows:

The boy's father, Dennis, was a strapping, robust man known for his incredible appetite, which I witnessed firsthand when he proceeded to eat one dozen pancakes for breakfast one morning! However, his stomach was no match for little Terrance, who ate over 20 pancakes, then asked for more!

Terrance's hair was another oddity. His poor mother would cut it every morning, only to have it grow several inches by day's end. Brushing and combing the hair proved useless as it always grew at odd angles and stuck up like a pineapple.

Note the pointed ears.

He was always snickering but barely ever spoke.

—11—

Always barefoot

Hamadryas nemorivagans

ÆLVEN CHANGELING

RENDERED ONE-FIFTH ACTUAL SIZE

In certain light, Terrance's eyes were an icy blue. Other times they appeared a deep, dark green.

will also eat differently from a regular child. Although they can consume enormous quantities, some are very picky and occasionally refuse to eat anything but uncooked vegetables or flowers. Their hair and nails grow long quite quickly, adding to the strangeness of the changeling's overall appearance. Perhaps the unnaturally swift growth is due to the difficulties with aligning a human body to a faerie passage of time.

The fey folk cry and laugh at inappropriate times and say unexpected and strange things. A person that speaks entirely in singsong or riddles is probably a changeling.

The changeling boy was prone to long walks in the woods, where he would disappear for hours on end (even in the middle of the night!). Eventually he went missing and was never seen again.

Several months later, a bundle of strange fruit appeared on the Finks' doorstep, wrapped in the boy's shirt. I told them to dispose of the fruit immediately as it was no doubt tainted.

Copse of trees near the Fink farm, probably an enchanted area

Changelings have been known to try to lure their human "family" into the hands of their faerie family. Beware if asked to go on a moonlit walk through the woods with a family member that has been behaving strangely.

To win back your stolen family member, you should catch the changeling and return it to the faerie mound where it came from. If this proves impossible, you can threaten the changeling with iron, which has the same effect on changelings as it does on all creatures of the Invisible World. Although in some of the old stories the changeling is thrown on a fire or burned with a hot poker, it is unlikely that such an action would go unpunished.

Occasionally a changeling will grow up with a mortal family and his or her odd characteristics will diminish, until even the faerie forgets that it is not human. (Compare to pixie, p. **14**, and elf, p. **31**.)

Pixies

FAMILY: PUSILLIPRAEDONIDAE

Tricksy by nature, *pixies* particularly delight in tormenting humans. For this reason, they can be found living in suburban and rural areas, and sometimes even in the parks of cities, any greensward, basically, where people frequent.

Ranging between two feet and the height of a human child, pixies (also known as *piskies*) make their homes in the hollows of logs, lean-tos formed by felled trees, and in gardens. Unlike boggarts and brownies, pixies never live inside houses, preferring to dwell outdoors. They sometimes can be spotted alone but are more commonly found in groups of three to five. Their desire to dwell in groups place them in the trooping category within the Invisible World.

Due to their prankish nature, pixies are unremarkable in coloring. Their clothing is usually natural in tone, all the better for hiding themselves as they wait for someone to fall into their next trap.

Like many faeries, pixies dislike rude, greedy, and cruel people and often single them out to be the victims of their pranks. Pixies are particularly known for knotting hair, leading people astray, and pinching skin black and blue. Pixies also have a fondness for stealing horses.

An excellent sign of pixie presence is small items going missing. Of particular interest to pixies

~ Have you ever been under a magnificent oak tree only to get hit in the head with an acorn? Chances are that a mischievous pixie was to blame.

PLATE V

Their clothing is composed
of dried grass, leaves,
and seedpods.

Wings seem to be more
prominent on the
juveniles.

This one was fascinated
with my artist's tools and
swiped one of my brushes.

These shoes were likely
"borrowed" from
a leprechaun.

Hamadryas compensis
FIELD PISKIE
RENDERED ONE-FOURTH ACTUAL SIZE

Her eyes were a very pale green; her voice sounded like birdsong.

Her hair grew in brown and green stalks that imitated thatch.

She was about the size of a human child.

The leaves of her dress were a drab green with rusty brown blotches.

May 1st, 19—

I spied a female in an old field dancing about in the grass. As she spun around, small seeds fell from the leaves of her dress.

Noticing my presence, she stopped and studied me, seemingly curious. I told her that I meant no harm and that I was only there to observe and record.

She stared at me for some time and said, "You have come too far. Your destiny is forever changed." With that, she transformed into a dragonfly and flitted away.

Her feet were stained a deep green from dancing in the grass.

In an area where there are pixies,
you may spot small harnesses on
foxes and on other medium-size animals.

are thimbles, pincushions, toothpicks, eating utensils, paper
clips, and straight pins. If you are lucky enough to discover
a pixie's lair, you will be surprised at the array of things
they've "borrowed."

If a dog barks for no reason while staring at an empty spot
along a fence or a cat chases something unseen in a garden,
it is very likely that the yard in question is infested with
pixies. There is, however, a way to be sure. Simply take a
clod of grassy dirt and turn it grass-side down. If, when you
return later on, it has been flipped back, there are definitely
pixies in the area. (Compare to brownies, p. 3; boggarts,
p. 6; and stray sod, p. 21.)

This very old butter churner was
discovered in an open field full of
goldenrod. Upon lifting the lid, I
found it to be full of items swiped
from my house.

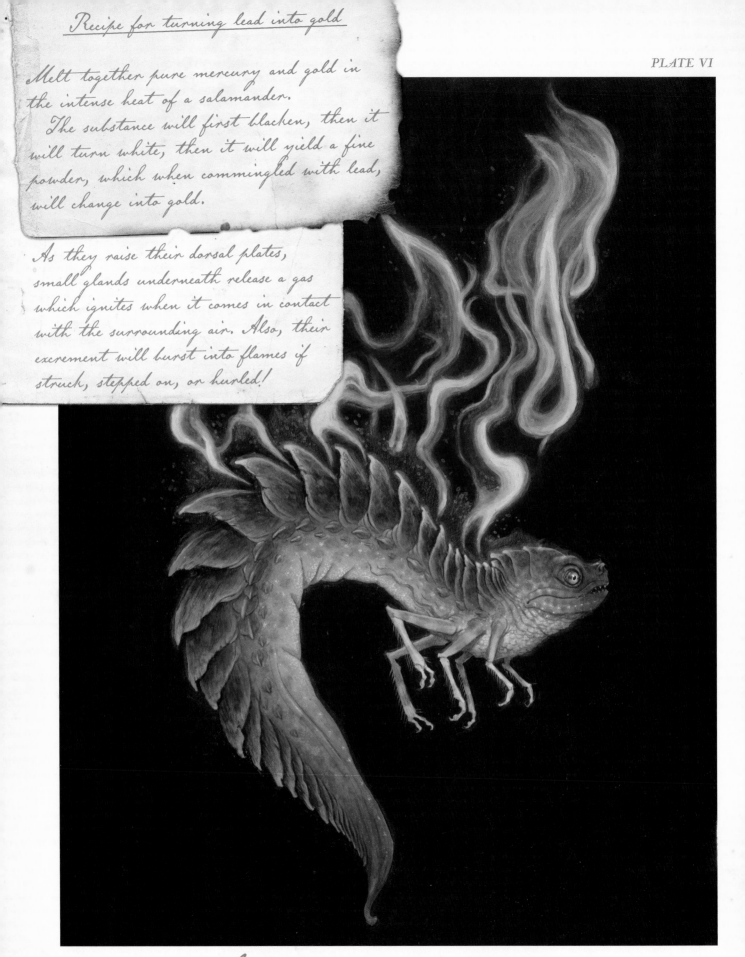

PLATE VI

Recipe for turning lead into gold

Melt together pure mercury and gold in the intense heat of a salamander.

The substance will first blacken, then it will turn white, then it will yield a fine powder, which when commingled with lead, will change into gold.

As they raise their dorsal plates, small glands underneath release a gas which ignites when it comes in contact with the surrounding air. Also, their excrement will burst into flames if struck, stepped on, or hurled!

Salamander flammulaticus

FIRE SALAMANDER

RENDERED TWICE ACTUAL SIZE

Could these creatures be the juvenile form of dragons?

Salamanders
FAMILY: FLAMMIEUNTIDAE

The *salamander* is a tiny, deceptively agreeable creature resembling its amphibious namesake. It can withstand extreme heat, and when threatened, the salamander will ignite, creating a white-hot flame around its body. Regardless, its skin is cool no matter how hot the temperature around it.

The flaming salamander can be found in damp places or in woodpiles, although it has also been spotted near volcanoes. It gives off the odor of sulphur and is believed to secrete poison so terrible that it burns whatever it touches.

Salamanders are sought by alchemists because they are an integral component for turning lead into gold. They are also sought for their pelts, since the skins can be used to make flame-retardant gloves. Although swift, a salamander can be caught with tongs and kept in an iron box.

~ Sometimes an unknowing salamander gets brought in with a bundle of firewood from outside. Agitated from having its home disturbed, it can ignite the entire fireplace in one instant! You will see it swimming among the white-hot flames until it vanishes up the chimney.

If you touch a match to a salamander's back, the match will light.

~19~

PLATE VII

This specimen hopped about in a clumsy fashion and was sighted in a pasture.

Note the smaller secondary eyes.

A. Spiderwick

They can be bright green like a treefrog, or a drab brown like dead grass and can change color at will, much like a chameleon.

Caespes ridiculus

WANDERING CLUMP

RENDERED ACTUAL SIZE

Stray Sod
FAMILY: HERBIFORMIDAE

The *stray sod* is a troublesome creature whose entire purpose seems to be leading travelers astray. These faeries wander about in open fields and grassy areas and can occur in large numbers. Many consider the stray sod to be a subspecies of the pixie. Others suppose that stray sod are not pixies at all but are created by pixie magic. If this is so, it is unclear if stray sod are aware of their effect on humans.

If a human inadvertently steps on stray sod, that person loses all sense of direction. The disorientation takes effect the instant a foot is placed on the creature's back and lasts for hours. Victims have been known to wander around their own neighborhood with no hope of finding their way. Landmarks appear missing or in the wrong places, roads look unfamiliar, and everything is strange. People have even become lost in their own front yards.

Eventually the effect wears off; however, the spell can be broken immediately by turning clothing inside out or by carrying a piece of bread in a pocket.

-21-

They are less intelligent than pixies but just as cunning.

This is the position of a stray sod at rest, showing grass-like growth on its back, which serves as camouflage.

PLATE VIII

Head and face
variations

Caespes aberrans
STRAY SOD
RENDERED TWICE ACTUAL SIZE

PLATE IX

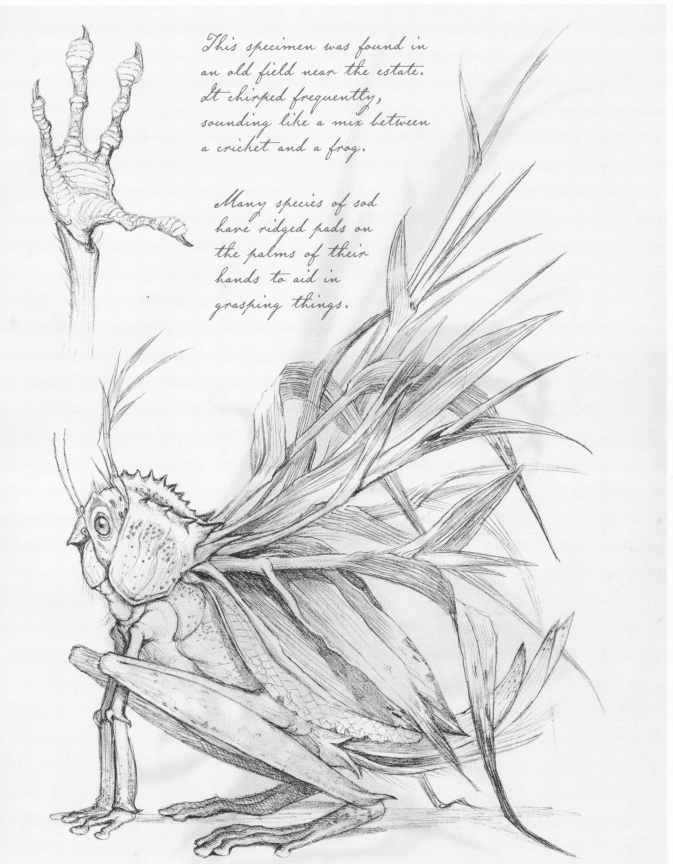

This specimen was found in
an old field near the estate.
It chirped frequently,
sounding like a mix between
a cricket and a frog.

Many species of sod
have ridged pads on
the palms of their
hands to aid in
grasping things.

Caespes insignificans
STRAY TUFT
RENDERED TWICE ACTUAL SIZE

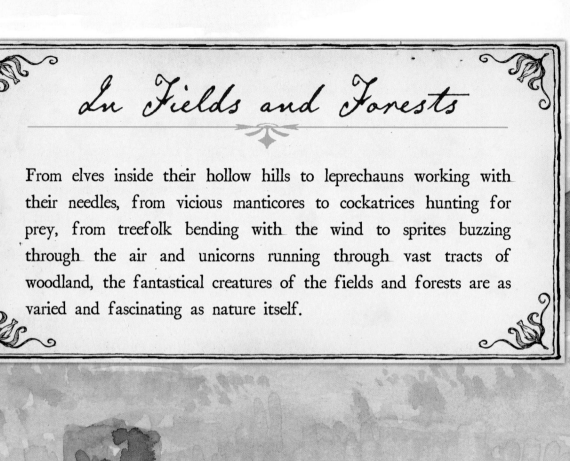

In Fields and Forests

From elves inside their hollow hills to leprechauns working with their needles, from vicious manticores to cockatrices hunting for prey, from treefolk bending with the wind to sprites buzzing through the air and unicorns running through vast tracts of woodland, the fantastical creatures of the fields and forests are as varied and fascinating as nature itself.

Watercolor sketch looking south across Dulac Drive

July 15th, 1921

Cockatrices
FAMILY: SERPENTIGENTIDAE

The *cockatrice* can cause death with a single glance. Reports indicate that anything catching sight of the lethal bird's eyes is turned instantly to stone. But just as deadly is their poisonous saliva, which can fell even an elephant.

Also known as a *basilisk*, a cockatrice has the head and feet of a cockerel and the tail of a serpent. The cockatrice is believed to be the product of a seven-year-old cockerel's egg, laid during a full moon and then hatched for nine years by a serpent or a toad.

There are a few ways to protect oneself from a cockatrice. One is to carry something reflective — like a mirror — and turn the creature's gaze back on it. Another is to keep either a weasel or cockerel nearby. The weasel is said to be the mortal enemy of the cockatrice, but the crowing of the cockerel is even more effective, causing the cockatrice to have fatal fits and to thrash itself to death.

-26-

This peculiar rock is believed to be a field mouse that was petrified by the deadly gaze of a cockatrice. (It was found on the same farm as the dead cockatrice.) When I showed this to the rancher who owned the farm, he produced a cigar box full of stony mice.

from
"Theatrum universale
ominum Animalium"

December 10th, 1915

Reproduction of a 15th-century
woodcut from Nuremburg, Germany

[overleaf]
Full-size drawing of a cockatrice done
from a dead specimen found on a local farm

FALSE COCKATRICES

Even in the Invisible World, mimicry
exists. Note the lack of horny growths
on the heads of these fantastical cockerels.
This is the key feature in differentiating
between these and true cockatrices. Their
feathers mimic the dangerous creature,
and predators leave them alone.

They have forked,
serpent-like tongues.

Head showing
frill relaxed

A. Spiderwick

s europeanus
COCKATRICE
-THIRD ACTUAL SIZE

Detail of foot showing avian features, including a fighting claw/spur

This is how I imagine its warning stance, with its bright, colorful neck frill fully extended and its feathers ruffled.

Reconstructed from a dead specimen

Basiliscu EUROPEAN

RENDERED ON

On the property across from ours, I have discovered a small band of elves living deep within one of the wooded areas. Shy by nature, they have taken some time to get accustomed to my daily presence.

I've spoken with several of their tribe, and have even coaxed a few to pose in trade for some of my drawings.

In fact, they seem particularly interested in the field guide I am creating.

It would seem that one of the elven elders, a fellow named Lorengorm, is distressed about the contents of the Guide and has forbid any of the other elves to accommodate me and my studies.

I will continue forth in the hope that we can reconcile once the book is completed.

Her hair was a whitish blond and finer than any hair I'd ever seen before.

This individual was recorded in the early spring months.

A. Spiderwick

Approx. 400 years old

Dryas nemorivagans
WOOD ELF (FEMALE)
RENDERED ONE-SIXTH ACTUAL SIZE

Elves
FAMILY: CIRCULIFESTIDAE

Elves are capricious by nature, and few rules govern their long lives. They are fond of circular dances, feasting, singing, and gaming and are most likely to be spotted when engaged in one of these activities. Sometimes, for amusement, elves will lure humans into dancing with them or tasting some of their food. In both cases, the humans will lose all track of time and be trapped unless rescued.

If one hears music coming from seemingly uninhabited woods or from underneath hills, chances are the area is inhabited by elves. Elven music is thought to be the source of many great human compositions, but hearing it can also bring on madness.

When walking through the woods, one should pay special attention to hills that are ringed with thorns or are close to streams. Walking around such a hill, one might notice places where the ground is sunken. Travelers should beware these hollow hills, as they are likely to be the dwelling places of elves.

Elven skin is pale and translucent. It peels in leafy, petal-like shapes, which change color with the seasons. This "petaling" appears on both sexes and seems prominent on the limbs, chest, forehead, and shoulders.

Most elves adorn themselves in clothing that is comprised of forest materials. Along with the tone of their skin, their wardrobe will also change color with the seasons. Many start with washed-out, pastel colors during the colder months and deepen into rich, saturated hues by late fall.

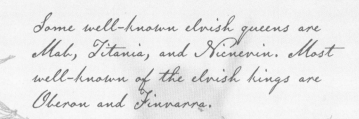

Some well-known elvish queens are Mab, Titania, and Nicnevin. Most well-known of the elvish kings are Oberon and Finvarra.

Elves are governed by regional monarchies where the queen has greater authority than the king. Each "court" is said to be either Unseelie (if composed primarily of malevolent elves) or Seelie (if composed primarily of benevolent elves).

The monarchs lead mounted parades on May Eve, Midsummer Eve, and November Eve. Although people do sometimes see these trooping elves, more often the only evidence is a strong wind that sweeps past and disappears.

~ *Elves sometimes enchant grass around their mounds so that anyone stepping on it becomes disoriented and walks away from the hill.*

PLATE XII

He was over 500 years old.

He smelled faintly of damp leaves.

The males seem to be more colorful than the females, especially late in autumn.

This is Lorengorm, an elven guard. He was very wary of my presence.

His armor seemed to be composed of dried leaves and seedpods.

His bow was made from an unknown wood.

RENDERED ACTUAL SIZE

Elfshot found buried in a tree

~ Elfshot is one or more thin, triangular pieces of black stone that are the only evidence left behind by elven bows. These are deadly in combat, burrowing their way into an opponent's heart.

A. Spiderwick

Dryas nemorivagans

WOOD ELF (MALE)

RENDERED ONE-SEVENTH ACTUAL SIZE

PLATE XIII

This chap's name was Allister Sassafeas. He lived in a nearby field where he would make single shoes.

Grass tucked in his hat contributes to camouflage while working.

His large ears allow for exceptional hearing.

This shoe is made from dried and treated leaves.

Buckles on his shoes have sharp prongs, used as spurs whilst riding livestock.

Cobblers' tools always handy

A. Spiderwick

Sutor vetus
OLD-WORLD LEPRECHAUN
RENDERED ONE-HALF ACTUAL SIZE

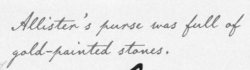

Allister's purse was full of gold-painted stones.

Leprechauns
FAMILY: INGENIOSIDAE

Leprechauns (also sometimes called *clurichauns*) are the diligent craftspeople of Faerie, tirelessly toiling at leatherworking and cobbling. They spend most of their time in their forest workplaces, although they do sometimes winter in the cellars of human homes, particularly ones where food is stored. Many people have entered their basements in the spring to find shelves filled only with empty cans and bottles because of a leprechaun.

Although known for their incredible shoemaking skills, leprechauns have a variety of other talents, including tailoring clothing, building homes, and fashioning tools. They can forge horseshoes and will sometimes shod unusual beasts, such as goats and the occasional cat. They may also ride these animals as though they were steeds.

Leprechauns are known for possessing gold they earn through their craft and must often employ a host of tricks to keep

~ 35 ~

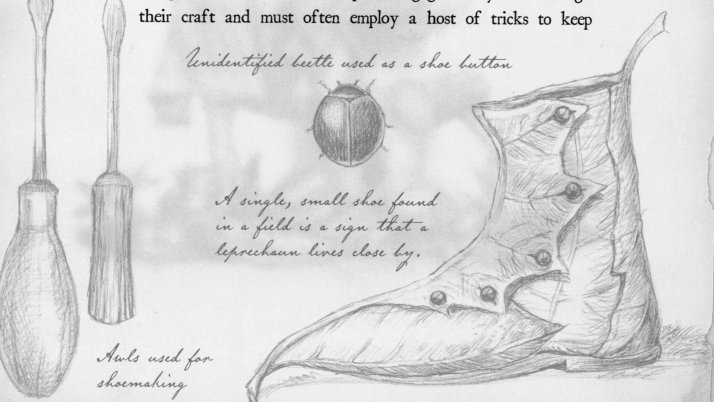

Unidentified beetle used as a shoe button

A single, small shoe found in a field is a sign that a leprechaun lives close by.

Awls used for shoemaking

This is Allister's brother, Bernie. Although solitary in nature, leprechauns will sometimes live in small groups.

~ Leprechauns will carry leather purses with "fool's gold" so that if they are mugged by humans, the robber will steal gold that will turn to ash at the next dawn.

Bernie gave me a handful of golden sunflower seeds. As I expected, by dusk the glamour had worn off and the golden luster was gone, revealing ordinary seeds. Surprisingly, however, when I split one open, I discovered a kernel of gold inside the shell.

Where leprechauns have spent time, clover is likely to spring up, particularly four-leaf clover.

This is a four-leaf mutation of RED CLOVER *(Trifolium pratense), caused by leprechaun presence.*

from being cheated, matching wits with their would-be robbers. One way leprechauns dupe thieves is by revealing the location of their treasure and then making sure it cannot be found again. If a thief marks the location by cutting a notch on a tree, he or she will return to find a similar notch on every tree in the forest. If a person digs a hole, they will find holes dug for miles around. And even if a leprechaun's treasure is obtained, if it is out of sight for a moment, it is likely to lose its luster. Gold may turn into leaves, and gems might become dull pebbles in a thief's pocket. And leprechauns, like other faeries, never forget when they have been wronged.

PLATE XIV

Manticores are only found in the deepest part of a forest. This one was drawn from memory. I encountered it while exploring rain forests in Latin America. I cannot even bring myself to write what it was dining upon.

It was surprisingly not as large as I imagined, perhaps the size of a cougar.

Quill from its tail

This individual was blind in one eye, perhaps as a result of a struggling victim.

A. Spiderwick

Note the poison gland, which continues to contract, pumping poison through the hollow spine, even after the spine has been expelled.

Martigor martigor
MANTICORE
RENDERED ONE-SEVENTH ACTUAL SIZE

Manticores
FAMILY: BESTIADAE

Originally documented in Persia, the feared, man-eating *manticore*, or *manticora*, has been sighted in places as varied as the jungles of Brazil and Indonesia and, more rarely, the forests of North America and Europe. With the body of a lion and a tail of poisonous spines that some reports indicate can be shot like arrows, a manticore is a lethal predator. It eats its victims whole, using its triple rows of teeth, and leaves no bones behind.

A manticore's face is said to resemble a human's, and travelers through marshes have reported mistaking a manticore for a bearded man from a distance.

Manticores have a melodious call, like the lower notes on a flute blown together with a trumpet. Despite the beauty of the sound, most animals know to flee when they hear it. Humans would do well to follow their lead.

~39~

October 13th, 1914

Drawing I reproduced from a woodcut done by a Topsell in 1607. The illustration seems quite literal d probably was not done from a live specimen.

- The food of a manticore mainly consists of large animals such as deer, antelopes, gazelle, and even humans. They will catch smaller mammals, such as rabbits, rats, or shrews, to supplement their primary diet.

Sprites
FAMILY: CORDIMUNDIDAE

Dazzling in color and about the size of large insects, *sprites* have glistening membranous wings. In fact, they are often confused with exotic insects or flowers at first glance.

Considered by many to be the most common type of faerie, they live in deep woods and make their homes high in the branches of trees. They particularly love to live in forests inhabited by treefolk and other fey. If sprites are spotted, you can be sure you are in an area with a high concentration of faerie activity.

Sprites travel in swarms and can bite if provoked. At night their bodies give off a faint glow that can have them mistaken for fireflies, which, along with other flying insects and small birds, they are fond of riding.

Petals and blooms missing from healthy plants may be due to sprites plucking them for clothing. Sprites can also cause plants to bloom in the middle of winter and are the nurturers of the strange fruits that faeries delight in.

In forests with sprites, you may find the hollowed-out acorns they use as cups, dandelion-tuft mattresses, and hats made from folded leaves. (Compare to will-o'-the-wisps, p. 115.)

Typical sprite head showing humanoid features with insect's antennae and eyes

Treefolk
FAMILY: HAMADRYADIDAE

FIG. A

Although all trees are magical and many are sacred to faeries, only a few trees are sentient. These are treemen and treewomen. *Treefolk* can take on a humanoid shape and move a short distance from their tree, or, in extreme cases, uproot the entire tree and use the roots as a shuffling form of locomotion. In their humanoid form, treefolk are often described as resembling their tree, so that an apple treewoman might have green hair and brownish skin while an elder treeman might have eyes as purply black as berries.

Obvious expression on the tree, composed of knotholes and strange permutations of the bark, is a sign that the tree may contain a spirit. Also check around prominent trees for roots that are above the ground. Lastly look for loose dirt and overturned moss.

Treefolk are likely to grow at the center of a faerie ring, to be a lone tree on a hillside or the oldest tree in a grove, to grow beside a welling spring, or to be one of two intertwined

FIG. B

~ Although treefolk are sometimes referred to as hamadryads, they differ from the Greek mythological beings in that they are not always young and beautiful nor are they always female.

FIG. C

FIG. A. APPLE (*Pyrus malus*)
FIG. B. AMERICAN MOUNTAIN ASH (*Sorbus americana*)
FIG. C. AMERICAN ELDER (*Sambucus canadensis*)

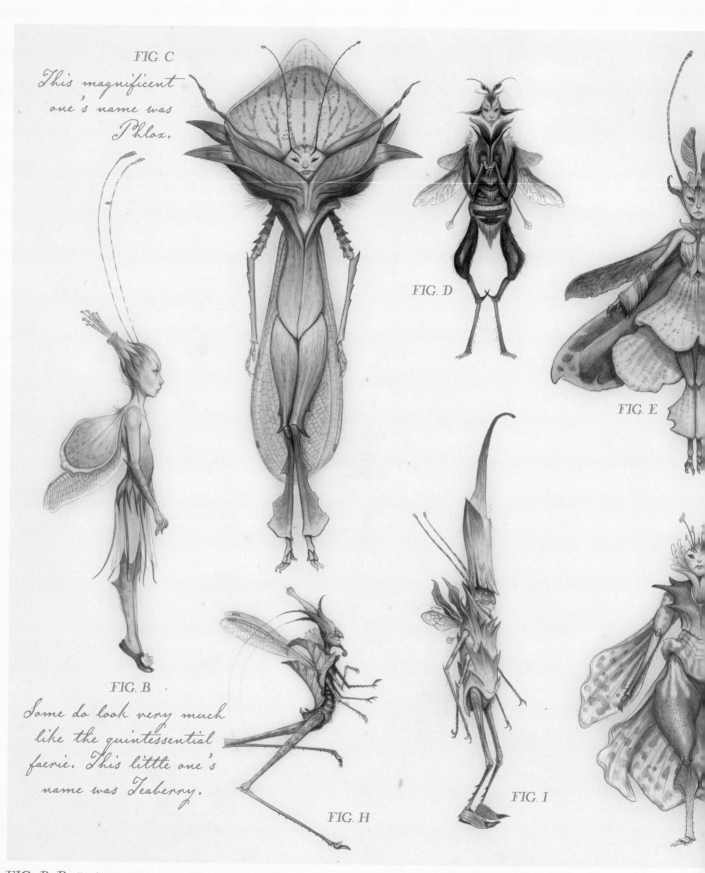

FIG. C
This magnificent one's name was Phlox.

FIG. D

FIG. E

FIG. B
Some do look very much like the quintessential faerie. This little one's name was Teaberry.

FIG. H

FIG. I

FIG. B. *Puella dumetae*, 48 mm
FIG. C. *Orchis regalis*, 81 mm
FIG. D. *Calæ diabolicus*, 23 mm
FIG. E. *Pinna papilionis*, 42 mm
FIG. F. *Corium ala*, 85 mm

PLATE XV

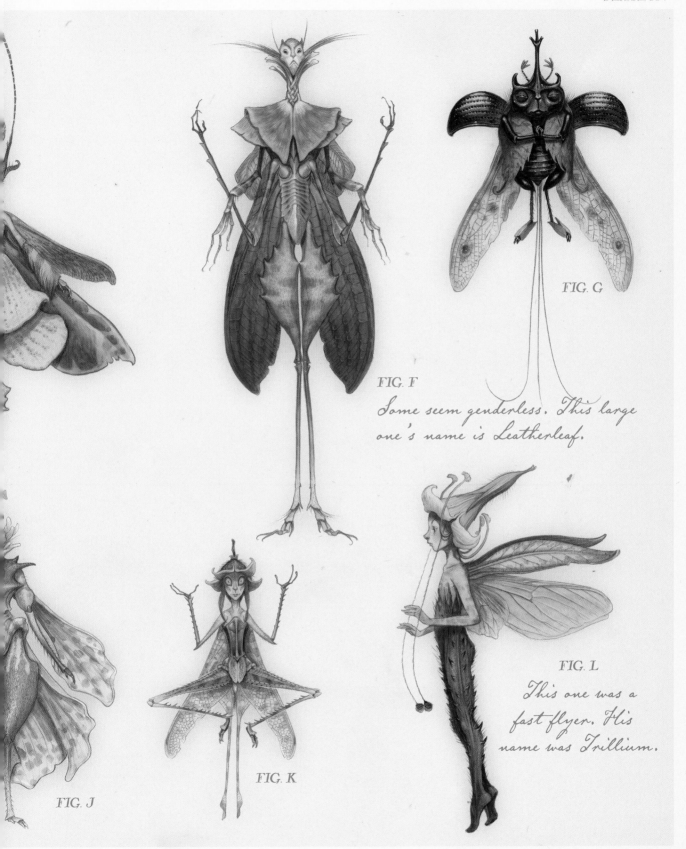

FIG. F

Some seem genderless. This large one's name is Leatherleaf.

FIG. G

FIG. J

FIG. K

FIG. L

This one was a fast flyer. His name was Trillium.

ST SPRITES

FIG. G. *Scarabaeus imitator*, 47 mm
FIG. H. *Gryllus barbatus*, 28 mm
FIG. I. *Surculigens*, 51 mm
FIG. J. *Orchis communis*, 45 mm
FIG. K. *Desultor agilis*, 32 mm
FIG. L. *Petasus floridus*, 45 mm

FIG. A *Ala florida*
This feisty fellow's name was Toadshade.
His armor was made from an insect's carapace.
size: 37 mm

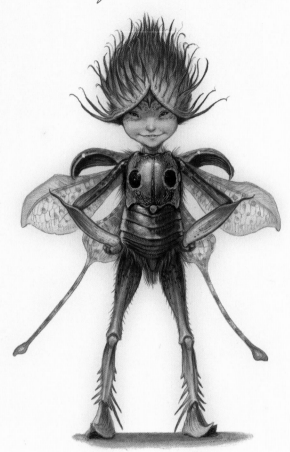

RENDERED TWICE ACTUAL SIZE

[overleaf]
I have encountered and recorded many different
sprite species. The following spread is done in hopes of giving a sampling
of their wide diversity in shape and form.

This ancient red maple spirit manifested in the form of a small child who never left the tree's shadow.

Her amber wings were very similar to a cicada's.

She never spoke directly to me, though I heard a whispery voice within the breeze as it ruffled through the leaves.

A. Spiderwick

Hamadryas aceris

MAPLE HAMADRYAD

RENDERED ONE-EIGHTH ACTUAL SIZE

This is a very ancient oak tree that I discovered deep in a nearby wood.

No other trees grew near it, and it was planted in a clearing full of wildflowers. It would not speak to me, despite my most earnest effort. However, no matter where I paused around its massive diameter, it still gazed down upon me with its gnarled eyes.

There have been accounts of disturbing effects when faerie fruit is eaten by humans. One wonders if these enchanted fruits grow from treefolk.

FIG. D

trees. Treefolk will die if they are cut down, although some linger on as spirits to haunt those that caused their demise.

Oak, ash, single thorn, and female holly treefolk are thought to be protective. Oak trees are particularly sacred to faeries and have the greatest likelihood of sentience. Of the protective treefolk, the most powerful is the mountain ash, also known as rowan. It may be considered so protective because of its red berries, which the female holly shares. Treefolk of these types are the most likely to be friendly in nature.

The holly treeman, by contrast, is considered malevolent. Also considered dangerous are hawthorn treefolk that occur in groups of three or more. Although elder trees are thought to be protective, their treefolk behave ambivalently. Elder treefolk are quite common. If blood-like sap seeps from their wood when it is cut, it is thought to be proof of their sentience.

Hazel treefolk are thought to be very wise and can impart wisdom to those that eat their nuts. Even eating the flesh of an animal that has eaten hazel nuts from a sentient tree is enough to gain wisdom. Likewise, apple treefolk are thought to give power and youth to those who eat their apples. Sleeping under an apple tree is a dangerous business, however, as one risks being carried away by faeries.

~47~

FIG. E

FIG. D. COCKSPUR HAWTHORN *(Crataegus crus-galli)*
FIG. E. WHITE OAK *(Quercus alba)*
FIG. F. AMERICAN HOLLY *(Ilex opaca)*

FIG. F

Horn I purchased from an estate sale in Germany.

The creature seems to be able to communicate through the horn with a form of extrasensory telepathy.

Unicorns
FAMILY: MONOCERATIDAE

Revered for centuries as one of the most magical of all creatures, the *unicorn* is perhaps best known for its healing qualities. The touch of a unicorn will cure disease and purify liquids. For this reason, unicorns were hunted and slain. Cups, plates, and utensils that could render poison harmless were carved from unicorn horns. Shoes and belts of unicorn hide cured fevers, and the ground-up liver of a unicorn was believed to heal leprosy. Even the powder of the horn was believed to cure a myriad of illnesses.

Named for the single, twisting horn on their brows, unicorns have slender, deerlike bodies, long necks, and tails that end in a puff of fur. Unicorns are solitary creatures, each one staking out a large tract of land and meeting only for the purpose of mating.

Despite their beneficent nature, unicorns are formidable when cornered. They are exceedingly fast and their horns are very sharp, making them a match for lions and even dragons.

Reproduced from a 16th-century woodcut

It has been written that unicorns will lie down for maiden girls. This is not the case and it is dangerous for anyone to approach a unicorn. Unicorns will only befriend those people of great innocence and purity of spirit.

Like zebras, they cannot be tamed or bear riders.

November 14th, 1917

According to some of the elder citizens, our little town has a regional record for lack of illness amongst its residents.

This, I now know, can be attributed to a unicorn living in a nearby wooded preserve.

Local hunters have described a great white stag living there, which, when encountered, gave them an overwhelming urge to leave the area.

I feel positive that this is a sign of the amazing beast.

A. Spiderwick

Unlike modern horses, they have toes, not hooves, similar to equine ancestors.

Unicornatus cristatus

UNICORN

RENDERED ONE-TWELFTH ACTUAL SIZE

In Lakes, Streams, and the Sea

From trolls and kelpies in their freshwater lairs to nixies in their streams and merfolk and sea serpents in the vast ocean, water faeries can be as fierce as the current and are often just as dangerous.

The lily pond at the end of Robinson Creek
July 20th, 1921

Kelpies
FAMILY: EQUIDAE

A ghastly water spirit that assumes the form of a grayish black horse, the *kelpie* drowns then devours anyone who attempts to ride it.

hind hooves:
15 cm long

It is often spotted wandering along the shores of rivers or lakes, appearing to be a lost pony. It can be identified by its constantly dripping mane and by its skin, which is like a seal's but cold to the touch.

The kelpie can be heard wailing before a storm and can cause water to rise high enough to flood.

If you manage to bridle a kelpie, it can be forced to do your bidding, but woe betide you should it slip its harness. (Compare to phooka, p. 113.)

One of my Icelandic correspondents wrote to me of a water horse called the nykur, which swims in the sea and whose hooves are reversed.

PLATE XVIII

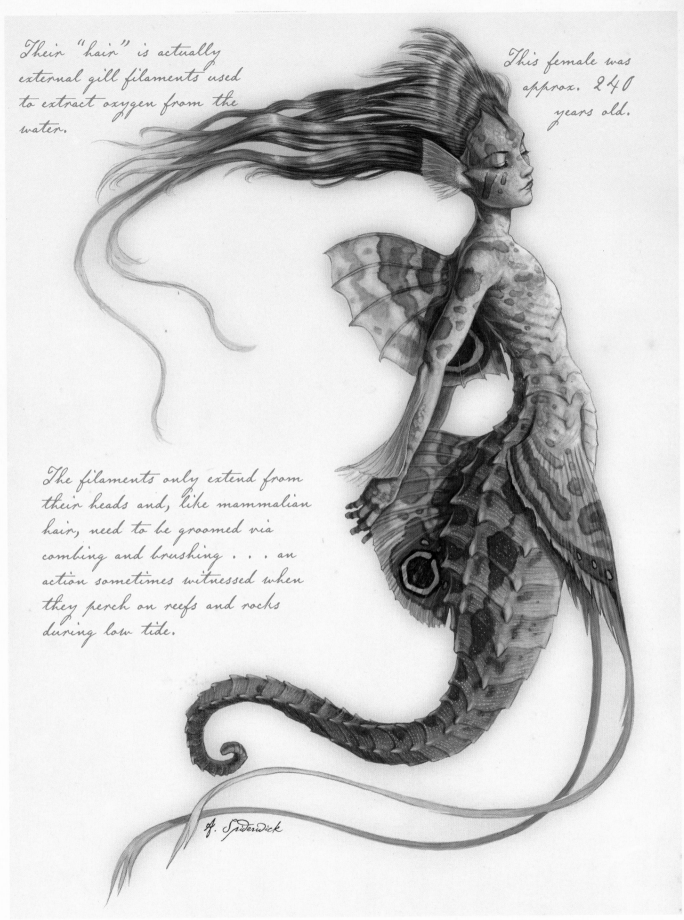

Their "hair" is actually external gill filaments used to extract oxygen from the water.

This female was approx. 240 years old.

The filaments only extend from their heads and, like mammalian hair, need to be groomed via combing and brushing . . . an action sometimes witnessed when they perch on reefs and rocks during low tide.

A. Spiderwick

Siren pacificus

PACIFIC SEA-MAID

RENDERED ONE-FIFTH ACTUAL SIZE

Dozens of sharp teeth line its muzzle.

Many times the eyes are hidden behind the shaggy forelock.

Equus ca
LAKE K
RENDERED ONE-EIG

Weeds and lily pads are ofte
knotted in its ratty mane.

A. Spiderwick

PLATE XVII

uivorus
ELPIE
ACTUAL SIZE

Many are about the height
and stature of a pony.

There were bleached bones scatterd about the
shoreline, a testament to past victims.

The track of a lake kelpie
walking in mud

You can clearly see the additional hooved
toes in its tracks. Like unicorns, kelpies
have a toe configuration more akin to
ancestral horses.

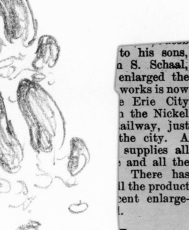

The stride is
approx. 55 cm,
a bit smaller
than a horse's.

to his sons,
n S. Schaal,
enlarged the
works is now
e Erie City
n the Nickel
ailway, just
the city. A
supplies all
e and all the
There has
ll the product
cent enlarge-

MILL.

of the Erie
of 11th and
prosperous
comprise a
mill being
with heavy
ipped with
ppliances,
me twenty-
d excellent

y g in reads of this firm is found in the
fact that they are steadily increasing their
business, and the future looks especially bright
for them.

SWIMMING HOLE GRAVEYARD

REMAINS OF CHILDREN FOUND
FOUL PLAY SUSPECTED

Dredging a popular swimming hole for traces of
two missing children resulted in the discovery of
human remains. Although uncertain as to how
many bodies were found, police believe there are
too many to be attributed to natural causes. As
yet there is no word on whether Edith, 10, and
Peter, 12, are among the dead.

Many in the community report that the hole is a
popular place for swimming in the summers and
that they've even seen horses cool off with a
plunge into its waters.

Estima

Don't

W.

The On

M.

March 1st, 1929

My wife is increasingly troubled by what
she calls my "grisly and macabre" interest
in the recent spate of watery deaths. She
thinks I am becoming obsessed.

March 2nd, 1929

Perhaps my wife is right. The shifting
nature of faeries continues to confound
me. How am I to present my findings
to the scientific community and be taken
seriously?

I am no longer sure what is real and
what is illusion.

[overleaf]

Merfolk
FAMILY: SIRENIDAE

As stunningly gorgeous as they are dangerous, *merfolk* live in loosely structured kingdoms deep in the sea, but occasionally their natural curiosity causes them to come near the shore.

Although usually seen at night out on the jetties or even sometimes on the soft sand of the beaches, they have been spotted in daylight, resting on rocky outcroppings. They have also been found trapped in tidal pools when the sea changes.

Merfolk are at their most helpless out of water. Even though their dual-function lungs can breath air, their silvery scales dry out with overexposure to the sun.

Although merfolk are very beautiful, it is not safe to approach them. Land people and sea people have been at odds since earliest recorded memory. With pollution increasing and more aquatic species hunted to extinction, merfolk are even less likely to consider a land dweller as a potential friend.

-57-

Mermaids have no hair to speak of. Even what appear to be eyebrows are markings merely mimicking human features.

FIG. A. and FIG. D. *The hatched egg case of the* CLEARNOSE SKATE *(Raja eglanteria), often called a "mermaid's purse," and the* FLORIDA SPINY JEWEL BOX *(Arcinella cornuta) are used by merfolk to hold treasured possessions.*

FIG. B. and FIG. C. *The* SPINY SCALLOP *(Chlamys hastata) and* VENUS COMB MUREX *(Murex pecten) shells are used for grooming.*

FIG. A

FIG. B

Merfolk differ widely in coloration, sharing the distinctive characteristics of fish of their region. Male merfolk, known as mermen, are rare and solitary creatures except during the mating season. They can easily be distinguished from the mermaids by their larger size.

As with any culture, merfolk leave behind a significant amount of artifacts that can be found around their habitats. Small piles of discarded shellfish may well be evidence of a merperson coming ashore to dine. Sea people are unused to cooking, so there will be no sign of a fire and there may be some sharp object nearby that was used to pry the food open.

You may come upon sheets of seaweed drying along the shoreline. Merfolk weave a crude kind of fabric from it, called seaweed cloth, that is used for garments, rope, and even baskets.

~58~

FIG. C

FIG. D

Copied from a 17th-century woodcut

- Like certain species of tropical fish, merfolk may be capable of a physical transformation called protogyny, whereby a female mermaid can change herself physically into a male. The process allows the species to thrive and explains the rarity of male sightings. Whether they can change back to their female form remains to be determined. However, it has been recorded with various fish, so it is possible.

PLATE XIX

When relaxed, the spiny facial fins flow behind the head, covering the gill filiments.

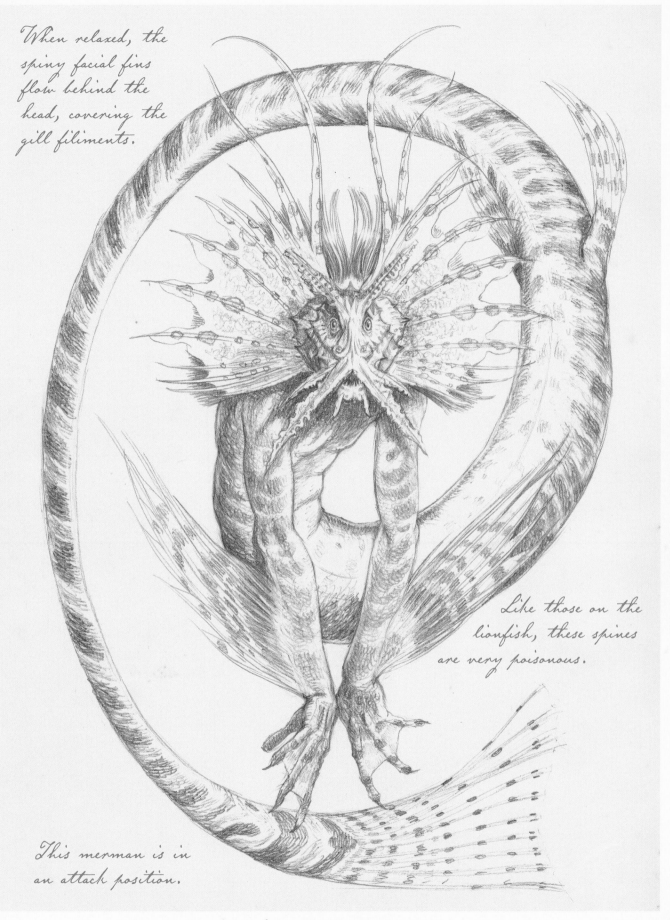

Like those on the lionfish, these spines are very poisonous.

This merman is in an attack position.

Siren atlanticus
ATLANTIC SEA KING
RENDERED ONE-FOURTH ACTUAL SIZE

PLATE XX

Like a sea anenome, her tentacled "hair" delivered a numbing sting to anyone foolish enough to touch it.

This mermaid had true gills, which opened and closed just below her rib cage.

This specimen could float perfectly vertical in the water with these swimmerets that ran up the ventral side of her tail.

Some individuals release an inky cloud from a sac located in their tail. They then swim off while the would-be predator is distracted.

A. Spiderwick

Siren caribbaeanus

CARIBBEAN MERMAID

RENDERED ONE-SIXTH ACTUAL SIZE

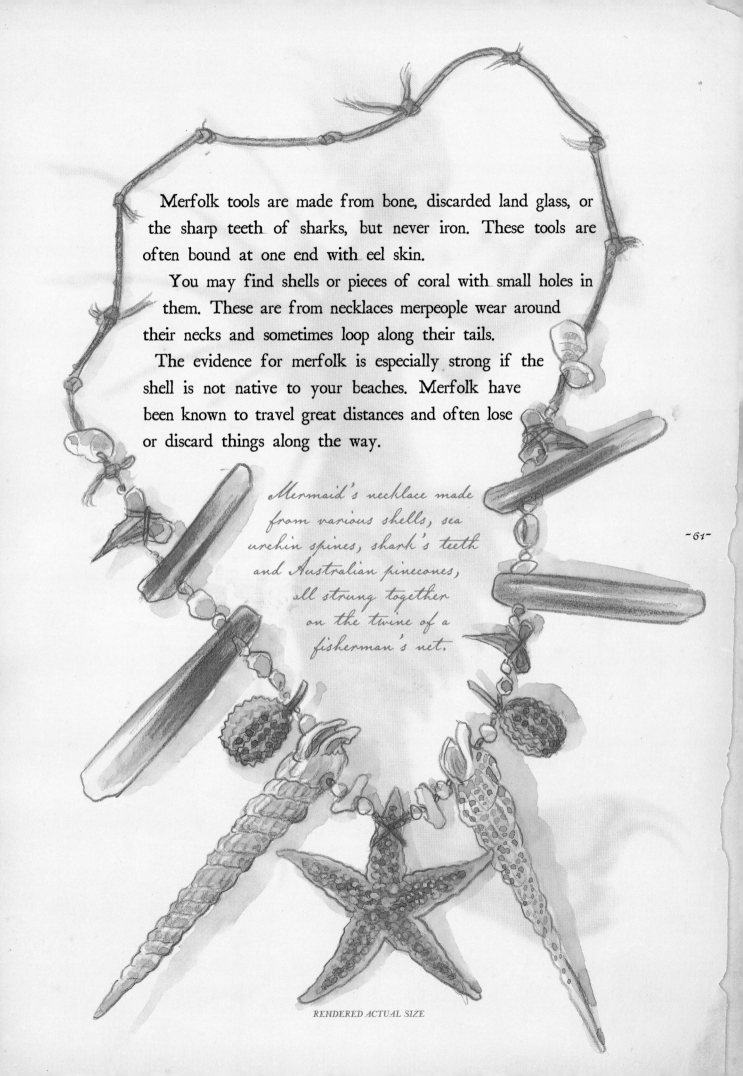

Merfolk tools are made from bone, discarded land glass, or the sharp teeth of sharks, but never iron. These tools are often bound at one end with eel skin.

You may find shells or pieces of coral with small holes in them. These are from necklaces merpeople wear around their necks and sometimes loop along their tails.

The evidence for merfolk is especially strong if the shell is not native to your beaches. Merfolk have been known to travel great distances and often lose or discard things along the way.

Mermaid's necklace made from various shells, sea urchin spines, shark's teeth and Australian pinecones, all strung together on the twine of a fisherman's net.

-61-

RENDERED ACTUAL SIZE

Like some merfolk, nixies have "hair" that is, in fact, external gill filaments that take in oxygen from the water as they swim.

They have no fingernails or hair to speak of, and their skin has a beautiful opalescent sheen to it, much like the soft underbelly of a frog.

I was able to get this one to pose for me by bringing our Victrola record player to the bank and playing music, which she greatly enjoyed.

Nixies have a translucent nictitating membrane that functions as a third eyelid and protects the eye while underwater.

A. Spiderwick

Nympha lymphae
FRESHWATER NIXIE
RENDERED ONE-FIFTH ACTUAL SIZE

Sea Serpents
FAMILY: SERPENTIMARIDAE

These scourges of the high seas are powerful and massive constrictors with flat heads, and bodies that coil around whales and ships, crushing their ribs. Unlike land snakes, however, *sea serpents* have many rows of long, sharp teeth. In the deep sea, they have been reported as growing to the length of a suspension bridge and are capable of creating maelstroms with the lashing of their tails and freak waves (sometimes called rogue waves or, ironically, monster waves) by surfacing close to a boat.

In shallower water, sea serpents may curl up and wait for prey. After coiling around an animal's legs, they will drag their victims out to sea. In deeper water, sea serpents usually swim in an undulating manner, like an eel, but certain species swim with their bodies vertical to the surface, disguising themselves as much smaller fish. This method allows them to dart up easily and swallow prey whole.

Crushed pieces of boats washed ashore are possible signs of a sea serpent. Look also for hooked teeth too large for a shark, or a long shed skin in the shape of a tube.

-64-

Shed teeth found on shore after a turbulent storm

[overleaf]

Like a snake, it has a flexible lower jaw that can stretch
to swallow very large objects. An adult sea serpent is
capable of swallowing a rowboat whole.

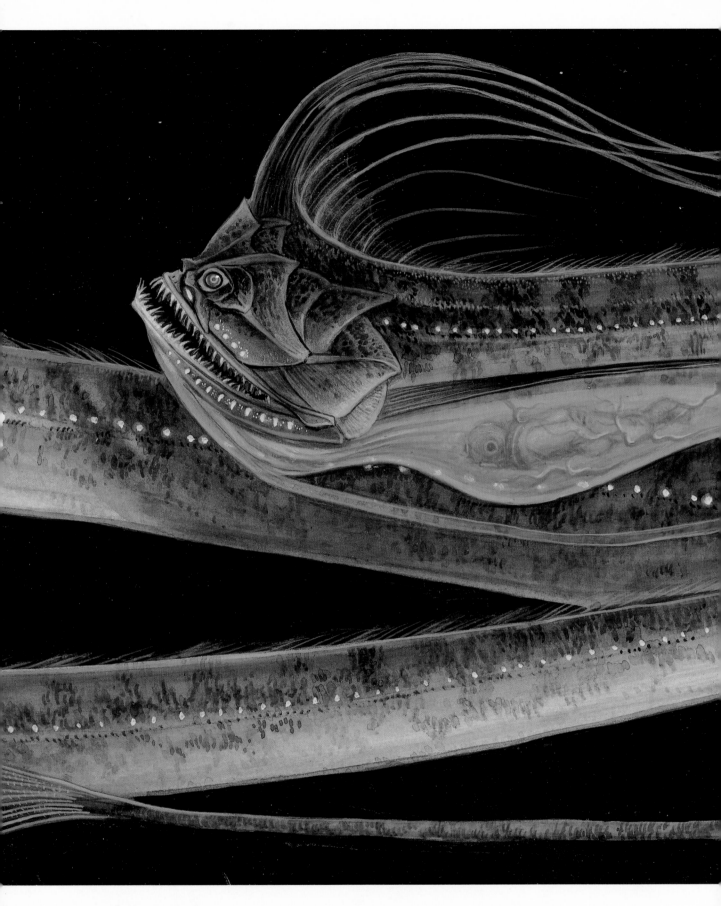

And, as you can see, this beast swallowed some poor deep-sea diver!

Serpens
NORTH ATLANT

RENDERED ONE-THIRTY-

- Waterlogged newspapers, books, and other items from the human world may be strewn around near their lairs. Also, clothes near a stream may belong to the nixie herself or to someone she has lured underwater.

Nixies
FAMILY: NAIADIDAE

Although I have heard of male nixies, I have only encountered females. I wonder if their gender variation is much akin to merfolk?

Guardians of freshwater pools and streams, *nixies* (also called *naiads* and *nixes*) are bound to the body of water in which they dwell.

They are most commonly spotted alone and can be identified by the liquid continuously streaming from their hair and clothes as well as the greenish sheen of their skin. Nixies are amphibious and, unlike mermaids, they have legs rather than a tail.

Nixies love music and dancing. Look for instruments made from reeds, especially pipes, near the banks of streams. Unlike their merfolk cousins, they are very curious about land dwellers. They are bound to their body of water and, much like treefolk may only venture a little way from their trees, can only venture a short distance from their pools. Therefore, they rely on other faeries to bring them information.

Occasionally nixies will lure a human into their pools, but they are usually more interested in company than in drowning their visitor. (Compare to treefolk, p. 44.)

Nixies are herbivores and have a natural affinity with their fellow pond dwellers.

A Monstrous Sea Serpent,

The largest ever seen in America,

as just made its appearance in Gloucester Harbour.

Cape Ann, and has been seen by hundreds of

Respectable Citizens.

and hung out his shingle, "Presque Isle Hotel." He erected a larger building the next year, moved to Walnut Creek. leaving his son Rufus S. to continue the business, which, under his able management, soon expanded to gigantic proportions and included general merchandise, grist mills, trading with the Indians, lake commerce, etc., etc.

The first vessel built in Erie was the Washington in 1797. Immigration had set in, a little settlement was formed, supply depots were opened, wharves were construct....... ness became active, and to create a .... only one essential was lacking—th........ sible journeyman printer hadn't ...... to start the "Presque Isle Weekly .... and Literary Repository." The firs..... in Erie was the *Mirror*, published ...... George Wyeth.

Erie was incorporated as a to........ a borough in 1833, and a ....

The first council conve.......

The Garrison Tract was the camping ground of the Pennsylvania militia in 1812-13.

Here in 1813, while the British fleet was drawn up in front of the harbor intent on destroying Perry's fleet in course of construction at the foot of Sassafras and Cascade streets, and at a time when "Britannia ruled the waves" on ocean and lake, 2,500 soldiers were encamped on these grounds. They had cannon mounted, and such military display and military strength were here developed as .... ester should an entrance to the ....cious

Misery Ba...
vessel wa...
mainder ...
Centennia...

The An...
Commodo...
latter bei...

The Nia...
Erie Harl...

In Nove...
guarding...
Island, o...
threatene...
ñamed as...
a battery...
eral Brook...
and with...
trenchmen...
present bl...

At the ....
hamlet a...
west side...
opposite...
Parade a...
outlet wa...

French...
500 inhab...
creek, wi...
Their rel...
reversed...

Thos R...
peace and...
township...
counties),...
creek; and...
de Chartre...
Phillippe,...

A vessel...
35 tons, w...
creek, in...

It was...
"Fallen T...
August, 1...
Indian tri...
ment of ...

General...
on the ...
tained at...
in length...

Sea serpents rarely come up from the depths to the surface during the day; usually it is at night, when they feed.

Copied from a woodcut by Matthaus Merian done in 1650 for "Theatrum universale omnium Animalium"

PLATE XXI

This magnificent specimen was observed off of the Atlantic coast, along the northern seaboard. Many local fisherman had reported seeing it the previous year.

marinus
IC SEA SERPENT
SECOND ACTUAL SIZE

Its skin was darker on the dorsal side and almost completely translucent at the underbelly and gullet.

Trolls
FAMILY: NOCTURNIDAE

Trolls are afflicted with a ravenous and never-ending hunger that leads them to devour whole flocks of livestock. In particular they have a taste for sheep, but they will eat whatever they can catch.

Trolls can survive extreme weather conditions and therefore tend to settle as far as possible from human settlements. Nocturnal by necessity since sunlight will turn them instantly to stone, trolls are more common far to the north, where it is dark for months at a time.

Water trolls live primarily in or near freshwater and usually make their home in a makeshift nest of rushes and mud along the banks of a bog or deep river. Bridges are also good places to build beneath as they provide shade even in the winter months.

~70~

May 4th, 1916

The previous owners of our new home have warned against letting horses graze too near the northern edge of the pasture, although they did not say why.

The area is lined with thick woods. Once I entered, I immediately discovered the cause of their concern.

The path went over a small creek via an old stone bridge.

Underneath, the tell-tale double humps of a troll sat in the watery shadow of the bridge. I will have to demolish it to prevent further incidents.

Many are not as cunning as their ogre cousins, but they are very dangerous nonetheless.

PLATE XXII

Their lungs are large, allowing them to remain submerged for hours on end.

The hump and the top of the head, the only portions of the troll seen above water level, look like partially submerged rocks.

It smelled like a wet dog.

The small finger may be used for grooming.

These long arms are perfect for reaching over a bridge and grabbing passersby.

A. Spiderwick

Vorax flumineus
RIVER TROLL
RENDERED ONE-FIFTEENTH ACTUAL SIZE

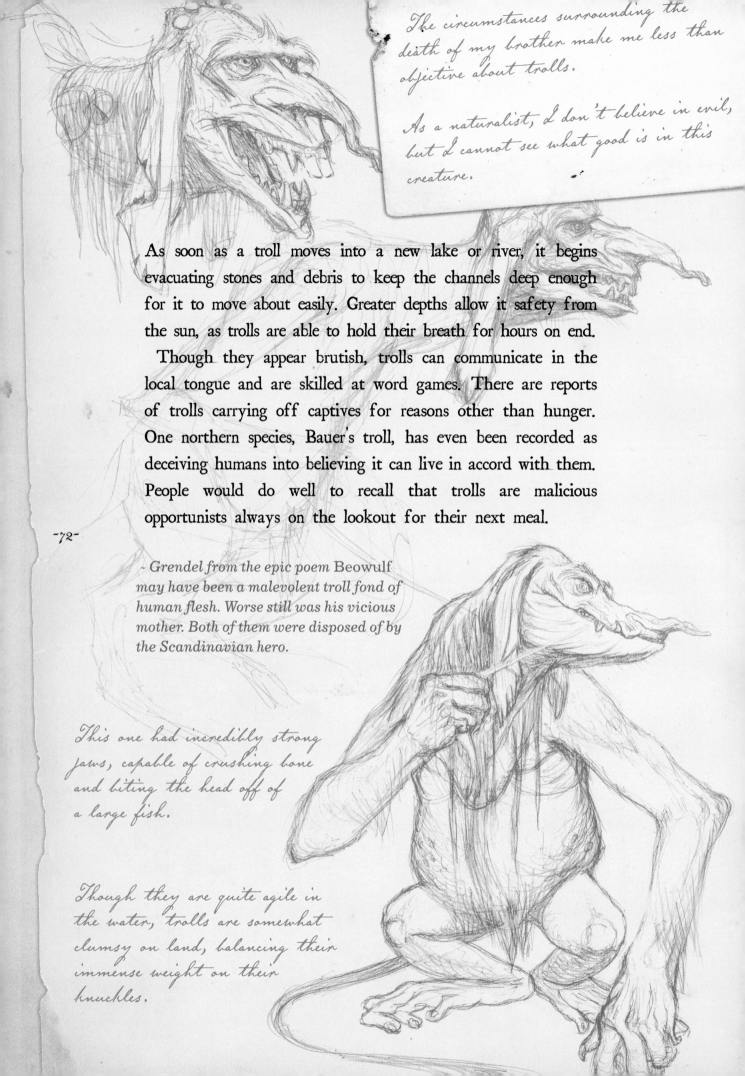

As soon as a troll moves into a new lake or river, it begins evacuating stones and debris to keep the channels deep enough for it to move about easily. Greater depths allow it safety from the sun, as trolls are able to hold their breath for hours on end.

Though they appear brutish, trolls can communicate in the local tongue and are skilled at word games. There are reports of trolls carrying off captives for reasons other than hunger. One northern species, Bauer's troll, has even been recorded as deceiving humans into believing it can live in accord with them. People would do well to recall that trolls are malicious opportunists always on the lookout for their next meal.

-72-

~ Grendel from the epic poem Beowulf may have been a malevolent troll fond of human flesh. Worse still was his vicious mother. Both of them were disposed of by the Scandinavian hero.

This one had incredibly strong jaws, capable of crushing bone and biting the head off of a large fish.

Though they are quite agile in the water, trolls are somewhat clumsy on land, balancing their immense weight on their knuckles.

All trolls have exceptional hearing and sense of smell.

This species will frequently leave its den and venture onto land in search of food.

Here, she has used the pelts from her meals as protection against the bitter, chilly environment.

This very old female was fond of shiny objects and had adorned herself with all that she had collected.

Note the shackles on her wrists. She obviously had been captured by humans at one point. Of course, in time the iron burned and calloused her skin.

She smelled like rotten wood.

A. Spiderwick

Vorax bavarensis

BAUER'S TROLL

RENDERED ONE-FOURTEENTH ACTUAL SIZE

In the Hills and Mountains

From giants as large as hills to dwarves that reside beneath them, from goblins and hobgoblins scavenging the land for food to knockers deep in mines and ogres in their abandoned estates, the faeries of the hills and forests are as old as the bones of the earth.

The hills looking north from Rountree Street
July 23rd, 1921

PLATE XXIII

His tiny eyes were used to low-light conditions.

This dwarf's name was Jarlite. He was as curious about me as I was about him.

Many have white beards, although black beards have also been recorded.

Much of their clothing is drab and earthen in color.

His skin was pale . . . almost translucent.

A. Spiderwick

Fosser borealis
NORTHERN QUARRY DWARF
RENDERED ONE-FOURTH ACTUAL SIZE

Mechanical
blooming-flower
rings

Dwarves

FAMILY: BREVIHOMINIDAE

Blinking-
eyeball ring.
The eye was
fashioned
from onyx,
sapphire, and
a diamond.

Dwarves are a diminutive race of faeries that live in mountains and deep forests. Since they are primarily subterranean by nature, most avoid bright light (including sunlight), and some are even nocturnal.

Young dwarves have a harsh, stonelike appearance that supports the theory they are carved from rock rather than born. As dwarves become older, their skin becomes finer and more polished, sometimes resembling marble. Dwarves can shift form to become a tree stump or stone, but if you look closely, you may be able to see their features in the wood or rock.

While the elves appear to behave like the aristocracy of faerie, idling away their days, dwarves are hard workers with strength far greater than their size. Like elves, however, they value bravery and loyalty and will punish those that ridicule or trick them.

Mountain climbers will sometimes find rings or other odd items along ledges or in shallow caves. They may also occasionally hear the clanging of these eternal laborers.

Master craftsmen, dwarves can forge any metal and make fine weapons that will never lose their sharpness. Because they lead very long lives, the death of other, less enduring things is a continuous source of sadness and many of their creations are an attempt to improve on nature.

This tiny clockwork
cave cricket was a
gift from Jarlite.
It is completely
automated.

Giants
FAMILY: GIGANTIDAE

~ Giants swallow salamanders and use their natural combustion to breathe fire. Hence the term "fire-breathing giant."

These lumbering brutes hibernate for most of their adult lives, sleeping for so long that their backs become densely forested. That, coupled with the fact that they can grow as large as hills and are often indistinguishable from the landscape, means it's entirely possible for a person to walk across the back of a sleeping giant and not even know it.

Highly territorial, giants seldom form attachments. Although normally placid, they can turn quite violent if roused. When giants take over new terrain, they will raze it to the ground, creating forest fires as a means of staking their claim. Giant territory is marked by unusual land formations: lakes in the shapes of footprints, trees knocked over without apparent cause, hills made entirely of dung, and boulders strewn where they were hurled in sport or fury.

-78-

Some giants hibernate in lakes, where they can absorb nutrients from the water. They are also capable of burrowing to locate underground aquifers.

PLATE XXIV

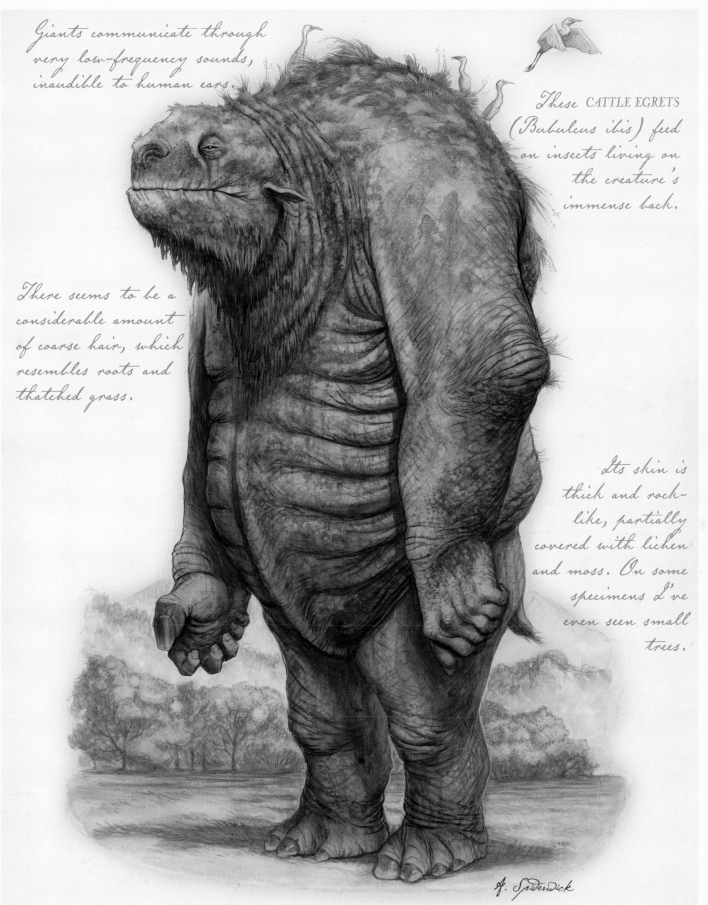

Giants communicate through very low-frequency sounds, inaudible to human ears.

These CATTLE EGRETS (Bubulcus ibis) feed on insects living on the creature's immense back.

There seems to be a considerable amount of coarse hair, which resembles roots and thatched grass.

Its skin is thick and rock-like, partially covered with lichen and moss. On some specimens I've even seen small trees.

A. Spiderwick

Gigas orientalis
EASTERN HILL GIANT
RENDERED ONE-FORTY-SECOND ACTUAL SIZE

PLATE XXV

Items used as teeth which I extracted from the gums:

A B C D E F

FIG. A. bird's talon FIG. B and E. mammalian teeth
FIG. C. glass shard FIG. D. sharpened wood FIG. F. pen nib

Goblins have acute hearing and a highly refined sense of smell.

Underside of hand showing opposable thumb

As masters of refuse, they will use anything discarded by humans.

Goblins urinate to mark their property and territory.

A. Spiderwick

Diabolus vulgaris
COMMON GROUND GOBLIN
RENDERED ONE-FOURTH ACTUAL SIZE

Goblins
FAMILY: ADENTIDAE

Malicious and grotesque, a single *goblin* is a nuisance, but in large numbers they can be quite dangerous. Goblins travel in roving bands that scavenge for food and hunt smaller prey. They make their homes in rocky outcroppings, caves, or even in ditches along the sides of roads.

Their pranks run from distasteful to depraved. The rare goblin that is mischievous but good-natured is known as a hobgoblin (see p. 85).

Most goblin species are born without teeth. They must find substitutes, either the teeth of other animals, or sharp objects like glass, rocks, or metals other than iron.

-81-

Some have bioluminescent organs on the tips of their tongues. These are used to attract sprites—their favorite food.

With its large mouth, it can swallow its prey whole.

May 12th, 1909

Bands of goblins can drive a brownie from its home if the numbers are overwhelming.

A little goblin lived under the floorboards of our home and was continually tormenting our cat (and even stole my inkwell!). Thimbletack finally disposed of it.

This spitting bog goblin has many extrasensory hairs, which act like whiskers.

There are many signs to look for if you suspect goblin folk are in the vicinity. Cats, dogs, and other small domesticated animals going missing is a telltale sign, as goblins will capture and eat them. Nightmares, especially of being chased, are another indication. For some reason, goblins have this effect on humans.

Certain types of goblin species haunt battlefields where many soldiers have fallen. They soak their hats in the blood of the slain and in that of their own victims. Appropriately, they are called redcaps.

~ In America there have been numerous recorded redcap sightings near the locations of Revolutionary War battles.

Dear Arthur,
    Considering what you told me of your studies, I thought you'd enjoy hearing some of the stories the boys at the Royal Air Force tell about a creature that interferes with the plane's mechanics. They call the chap a gremlin.
    One of the pilots told his writer friend, so I thought I might as well tell mine.
    Give my love to Constance. I will write to you again when I am back in the states.

            Cheers!
            -Robert

PLATE XXVI

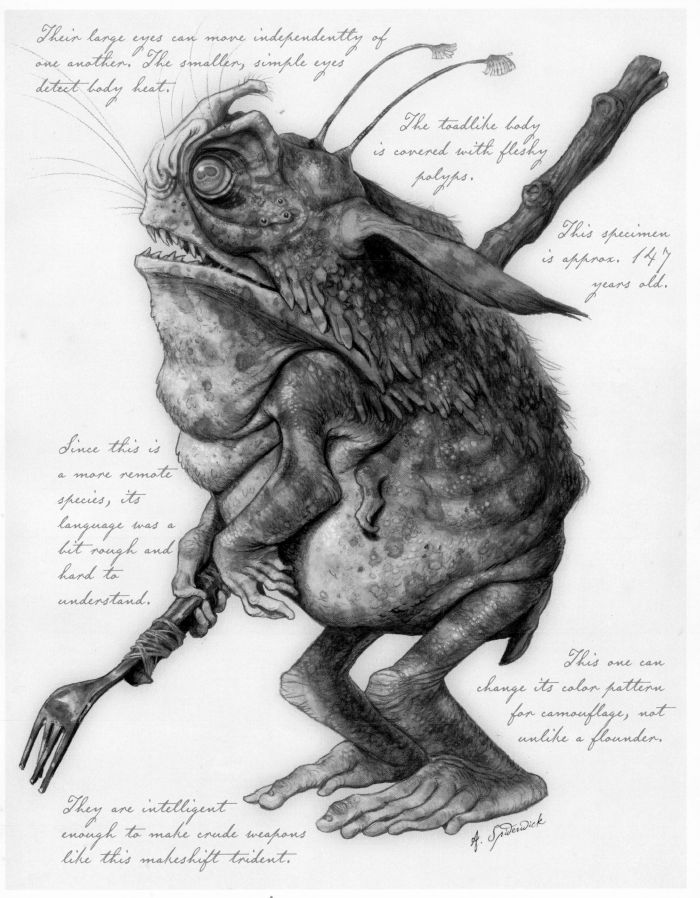

Their large eyes can move independently of one another. The smaller, simple eyes detect body heat.

The toadlike body is covered with fleshy polyps.

This specimen is approx. 147 years old.

Since this is a more remote species, its language was a bit rough and hard to understand.

This one can change its color pattern for camouflage, not unlike a flounder.

They are intelligent enough to make crude weapons like this makeshift trident.

A. Spiderwick

Diabolus invidiosus
GREATER BULL GOBLIN
RENDERED ONE-FOURTH ACTUAL SIZE

PLATE XXVII

This one's name was Piddledrip, and he liked to steal crayons and scribble all over the walls at night.

Like goblins, they have secondary eyes used for heat and motion detection.

Many have bat-like features such as large, fleshy noses and ears adapted for listening to high frequencies.

Also like goblins, hobs are born without teeth. Frequently they will steal teeth left by children for the tooth fairy.

Because they are primarily nocturnal by nature, they have incredible hearing and an acute sense of smell.

This one was also fond of urinating on the beds!

Diabolus praestigiator
COMMON HOB
RENDERED ONE-THIRD ACTUAL SIZE

Hobgoblins
FAMILY: AMICIDIABOLIDAE

Similar to goblins in appearance, *hobgoblins*, or *hobs* as they are sometimes called, are a less malicious and more mischievous type of faerie.

Friendly and sometimes even helpful, hobgoblins still have a penchant for pranks that can range from annoying to infuriating. They are most fond of stealing trinkets and food, but they also enjoy tripping people and otherwise causing amusing havoc.

Like goblins, hobgoblins are scavengers, but unlike goblins they are solitary in nature and are never spotted in large numbers. It is unclear if they are a wholly different species from goblins or merely the same species with a remarkably different disposition.

The mischievous Puck from William Shakespeare's *Midsummer Night's Dream*, identified himself as a hobgoblin.

Many times, children and pets are blamed for this creature's pranks and practical jokes. (Compare to pixies, p. 14.)

H. J. Ford's 1897 drawing of a hob for Andrew Lang's "Pink Fairy Book" is so detailed that one wonders if the artist may have had the Sight as well?

Their first finger is specialized for tapping on cavern walls.

The skin is translucent and covered in fine hairs like a peach. The ears can move independently, like those of a cat.

Knockers
FAMILY: CAVERNAHABENTIDAE

Also known as *kobolds*, these enigmatic creatures most commonly live in mines, mimicking the sounds of miners by tapping against the rock walls. It is said that they do their own mining at night when all the humans have departed, but since they do not appear to craft metal, it is unclear what they are seeking under the ground.

Knockers are valued because they will warn miners of impending disaster (like collapses) by pounding on the walls. Sometimes the pounding sounds like it's coming from all directions, alluding to a large number of creatures, but this may merely be a trick of the acoustics.

Knockers cannot abide whistling and swearing. They will cause small showers of stones to fall on anyone performing these actions or in other ways disrespecting them.

Outside of mines, knockers can be found in wells, caves, and sometimes even in basements. (Compare to brownies, p. **3**.)

Like their goblin cousins, knockers tend to collect human artifacts and find them fascinating.

These rocks were in a miner's coffee cup, found tied around the specimen's neck. The knocker called them "gob stones" and claimed they had magical properties.

PLATE XXVIII

Amicus auritus

DEEP CAVERN KNOCKER

RENDERED ONE-THIRD ACTUAL SIZE

Horn-like projections grow from their heads. The older individuals have a spectacular rack of horns.

Ogres
FAMILY: STULTIBRUTIDAE

Ogres often trade on their strength, despite having better than average intelligence. They live as scavengers, bullying humans and other faeries into giving up their food, land, and wealth. Luckily, ogres are both vain and lazy, attributes that often lead to their downfall.

Descended from giants, ogres are quite large in their natural form. They have the ability to shape-shift into creatures both smaller and larger than themselves, but they then share the strengths and limitations of each. In order to shift into a form, the ogre must have previously seen the creature it wishes to become, and it can only remain in that guise for a limited duration. In the fable "Puss in Boots," written in the eighteenth century, the clever Puss outsmarts one nasty, conniving ogre by convincing him to turn into a mouse.

Ogres are solitary creatures and it would be highly unusual to see more than one in the same place. Abandoned mansions, factories, hospitals, and other massive, isolated buildings may house ogres. They find such places more to scale for their size.

August 13th, 1927

I have met a particularly ancient ogre living to the west of town. He would not tell me his name; however, he did seem especially interested in the Guide. As with most of his kind, I am sure he is not to be trusted and I am severing contact with him.

PLATE XXIX

Flattery got this ogre, Balcorus, to pose for me.
He insisted on a formal portrait as opposed to
my "animal paintings."

Some ogres dress very
lavishly, others prefer
simpler attire. This
one was wearing a
silk banyan from
the 1700s.

He was fond of
griffin meat and
had adorned
himself with claws
and feathers.

Here he is holding a goblet made from a unicorn's horn. Many species
I found had six or seven digits on each hand and foot.

Horrifer perraultanus
PERRAULT'S OGRE
RENDERED ONE-NINTH ACTUAL SIZE

Watercolor sketch of our property looking east
August 5th, 1921

In the Sky

From poisonous dragons to fierce griffins and the glorious phoenix, the fantastical creatures of the sky soar through a realm barely glimpsed by humankind.

Dragons

FAMILY: DRACONIDAE

Formidable predators, *dragons* (also known as *wyrms* and *drakes*) are massive in size with fearsome teeth, deadly breath, vicious claws, and hides like stone. Dragons generally make their home in caves and mountains, far from humankind, but when they come close to people, their huge appetite is generally a source of conflict.

Dragons are fond of penned livestock; in particular they love to scrape the udders of cows and drink the milk. Milk accelerates the rate of a dragon's growth to an alarming degree. Their diet also includes large mammals and even big fish such as sharks. Occasionally, if driven by hunger, they will eat humans as well and have been known to lay siege to whole villages.

The last recorded dragon slaying was in the eighth century by the knight Sir Garrot. At that time, there were particular indicators that people used to determine if dragons were in the vicinity. These signs are still useful to keep in mind.

They include a thick, poisonous vapor in the air and water that stings the throats of those who drink it or burns the skin of those who bathe with it. Dragons exude poison and this poison seeps into everything they touch.

Like the snake, the dragon reproduces through laying vast quantities of eggs, few of which will hatch. Even fewer offspring live to adulthood. Dragons are solitary creatures and

For centuries many parts of a dragon's anatomy were used for medical cures and potions. Some examples include:

FIG. A

FIG. C

FIG. E

FIG. B

FIG. D

FIG. A. Dragon's blood will make one's skin as tough as armor.

FIG. B. If planted, the teeth of a drake will grow into soldiers.

FIG. C. The horns of a dragon can be made into instruments whose sound can carry over a great distance.

FIG. D. Eating the heart of the beast allows one to understand the language of animals.

FIG. E. If one were to eat the tongue of a dragon, one could win any argument.

Although these items seemed quite commonplace many years ago, they are no longer easy to come by.

April 20th, 1915

Today has turned out to be disappointing, and I realize I've made another trip out the west in vain.

The purported discovery dragon remains has turned to be nothing more than th fossilized bones of a dinosaur

September 17th, 1912

[overleaf]

With all of my talents and resources, I have yet to find any evidence of a living dragon. My fears of their extinction are becoming more and more a reality.

Therefore, I have created a representation based on exhaustive research and pure on the part of this author.

PLATE XXX

Many are covered in an odd mixture of
scales, feathers, and leather scales, giving
them an almost prehistoric appearance.

The bottom jaw is around,
allowing the tongue to
slide in and out quite
easily as it senses the
air around it.

Most wyrms are long
and serpent-like, and they can
move at an astounding speed.

A. Spiderwick

Can wyrms truly fly?

My guess is that they leap into the
air with great speed and writhe
through the sky the way a sea snake
undulates through the water.

Juveniles are brightly colored;
however, their coat darkens and
dulls with age.

Draco antiquissimus
OLD-WORLD WYRM
RENDERED ONE-NINTH ACTUAL SIZE

PLATE XXXI

March 14th, 1912

A specimen was spotted by a rancher while it was diving at his cattle.

I wondered how it was that he had the Sight (allowing him to spot the creature), and it turns out he was the seventh son of a seventh son.

This paddle on the tip of the tail may act as a rudder while the creature is in flight.

The dragon made a call starting with a hiss and ending with more of a warble.

Was it communicating with the farmer or others in the vicinity?

There were patches of fine down on its back and on the dorsal side of the wings.

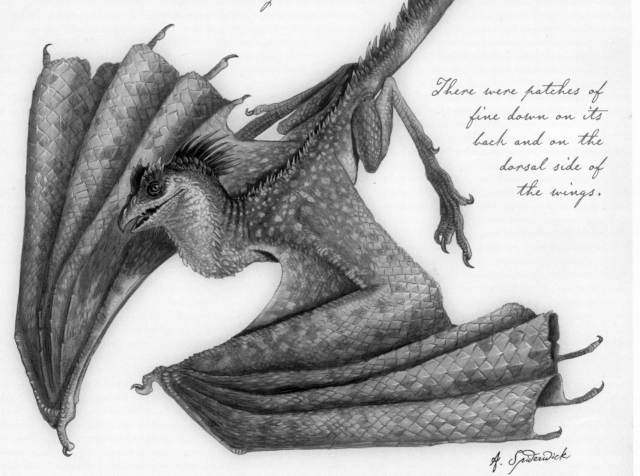

A. Spiderwick

Draco alatus

LONG-TAILED WYVERN

RENDERED ONE-EIGHTH ACTUAL SIZE

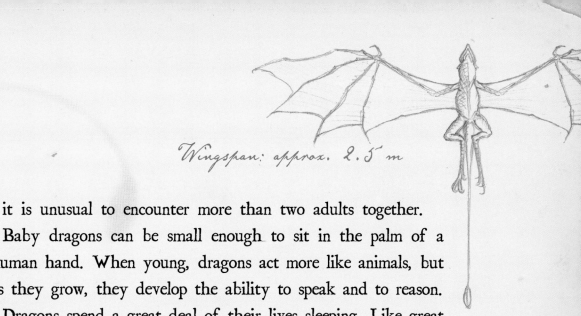

Wingspan: approx. 2.5 m

it is unusual to encounter more than two adults together.

Baby dragons can be small enough to sit in the palm of a human hand. When young, dragons act more like animals, but as they grow, they develop the ability to speak and to reason.

Dragons spend a great deal of their lives sleeping. Like great cats, they can appear lazy when not hunting. When moving with a purpose, however, dragons are swift, both on the ground and in the air.

Common the world over but especially throughout Asia and Europe, some dragons are known for their great wisdom, but reports of their guile are far more common.

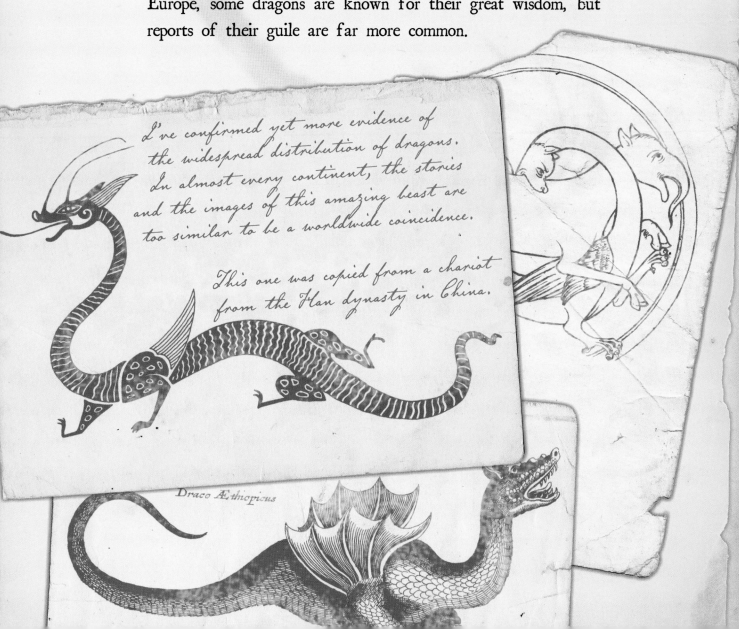

I've confirmed yet more evidence of the widespread distribution of dragons. In almost every continent, the stories and the images of this amazing beast are too similar to be a worldwide coincidence.

This one was copied from a chariot from the Han dynasty in China.

Draco Æthiopicus

Wingspan: approx. 4 m

Griffins
FAMILY: MIXTIDAE

The regal *griffin* (also spelled *gryphon*) is thought to be the offspring of an eagle (king of the air) and a lion (king of all beasts). Its plumage ranges from cream to deep brown, yet some specimens have feathers with a deep, dark bluish sheen.

While many griffins migrated to Europe from the Middle East in the thirteenth century, most remain desert-dwelling. They roost in high places and are only likely to be spotted when they fly in search of food. Their bones are more commonly discovered, although they are often mistaken for the bones of dinosaurs.

The adult griffin is about the size of a lion but far stronger. Despite their formidable natural advantages, griffins are very rare. Unlike less fantastical hybrids like mules, however, they can reproduce. Their eggs are said to be made of agate.

Griffins are resistant to the poison of dragons and very hostile to horses. For this reason, the offspring of a griffin and a horse—the *hippogriff*—is considered to be a symbol of the enduring power of love.

Egg redrawn from memory. I did not dare risk taking it from the nest.

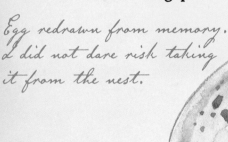

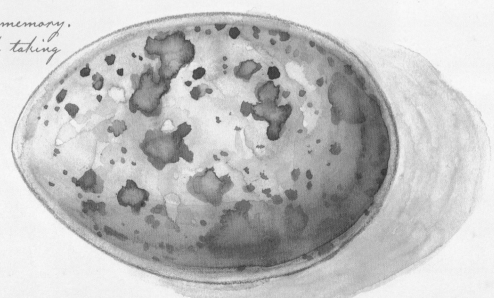

RENDERED ONE-HALF ACTUAL SIZE

-98-

PLATE XXXIII

The bright plumage would seem indicative of a male; but, upon closer inspection, I found the bird to be genderless.

Wingspan: approx. 1 m

Its call was the most beautiful I had ever heard, and its songs became longer and longer as the nest approached completion.

The nest was built from CINNAMON (Cinnamomun zeylandica), MYRRH (Commiphora myrrha), and SPIKENARD (Nardostachys grandiflora).

A. Spiderwick

Phoenix phoenix
PHOENIX
RENDERED ONE-THIRD ACTUAL SIZE

Gryphon americanus

NORTH AMERICAN GRIFFIN

RENDERED ONE-EIGHTH ACTUAL SIZE

Although the offspring of an eagle, this griffin had a head resembling a vulture or one of the more lightweight raptors.

This specimen lived in a very remote mountain range far north of civilization.

These
stereosco
they ca
miles a

A. Spiderwick

PLATE XXXII

...asts have amazing
...ic vision. In flight
... see a rabbit from
...ve ground.

The "mane" is a shaggy
mix of coarse hair and
long, thin feathers.

Their call sounds
like a screechy
tea-kettle whistle.

Like many fishing
eagles, they have
dangerously sharp talons.
Note the opposable,
thumb-like claw.

This one was quite fond of
catching SALMON (Salmo salar)
as they moved into streams to spawn.

Like dragons, griffins have been
recorded through stories and art in
many lands around the world,
indicating their vast distribution.

Described for centuries, this
beast has become more and more
majestic with each generation.

Flight feather
from nest site

[overleaf]

RENDERED ONE-THIRD
ACTUAL SIZE.

Egg sitting in the ashy remains of an adult. I wonder if the warmth of the ashes incubates it?

Phoenixes
FAMILY: VETUSTIDAE

The *phoenix*, sometimes called a *fenix* or *firebird*, is a majestic, glorious bird with purple and gold plumage. Custom says that there is only one phoenix alive at a given time, but the fowl is so rare that no one has been able to corroborate this notion. They do not require food to sustain themselves, though they have been known to eat the gum of the frankincense tree *(Boswellia thurifera).*

A phoenix will live for centuries (five hundred years, according to one source), whereupon it will build a nest of cinnamon, myrrh, and spikenard. There it incinerates itself by reflecting the sun off its plumage to spark a fire and fanning the flames with its wings. Nine days later, another phoenix hatches from those same ashes.

~105~

I went to dinner several nights ago at the home of a wealthy aristocrat from the city. While we were eating, a most wondrous birdsong emanated from the conservatory. Afterward I was shown the majestic animal and knew it at once to be a phoenix.

The owner did not know the bird's true identity, and thought it captured from the rain forests of Latin America. However, he did say that his family had owned it for as long as he could remember (probably for generations). It most certainly was a full-grown adult, and I am supposing it had not nested, for there was no access to the appropriate building material for it.

August 13th, 1918

I've convinced the aristocrat to have the bird sent here so that I may further study it. He has agreed, on the condition that I paint a portrait of his granddaughter in return. . . . Fair enough!

As I supposed, once supplied with twigs and branches of various spice-bushes, the phoenix hastily began building its nest.

What will I tell them when their beautiful bird is reduced to ash?

The eastern edge of our estate
July 5th, 1921

Outside at Night

From wailing banshees and gloomy gargoyles to tricksy phookas and will-o'-the-wisps that lead the unwary astray, these creatures make it obvious why humans have grown afraid of the dark.

Banshees
FAMILY: CIRCULIFESTIDAE?

Like brownies, *banshees* are loyal to their households, but rather than help with chores, these eerie and gloomy beings wander the grounds of estates, keening and washing the grave-clothes of those about to die.

Although banshees are described by some as beautiful and by others as hideous, all agree that there is something terrifying about the sight of one. There are even reports that a few unlucky people who have looked into the face of a banshee died of fright. The song of a banshee is similarly lovely and unsettling.

Some believe that preventing a banshee from mourning or refusing to listen to its song will delay death, but this seems unlikely as, in most cases, a banshee is not the cause of death but merely its herald.

Before the death of one of Albert's daughters, the banshee was seen carrying this doll and weeping.

August 17th, 1918

While visiting my friend Albert, I was warned to draw the drapes and not to open the windows under any circumstances. It being a warm and muggy night, I was puzzled, and I grew even more puzzled when I saw a white figure darting across the lawn.

I went outside and found a weeping girl. Her words made no sense to me and she would not tarry to talk.

In her presence, I found myself shivering from a chill that did not abate when I returned to the house.

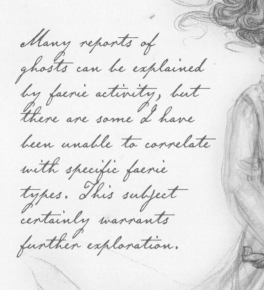

Many reports of ghosts can be explained by faerie activity, but there are some I have been unable to correlate with specific faerie types. This subject certainly warrants further exploration.

The banshee was spotted wringing blood from a wet rag in her hands. I found out later that the cloth was, in fact, the shirt of Albert's dying father. He and Albert's daughter both were victims of tuberculosis.

She floated above the ground at all times, hovering over an ethereal bucket and washboard.

Dryas styx?

BANSHEE

RENDERED ONE-EIGHTH ACTUAL SIZE

PLATE XXXIV

Series of sketches showing a gargoyle's hopping movement

I believe that they absorb their nutrients from rainwater through their porous skin.

They become quite active during storms, especially if they have been dormant for an extended period of time.

However, if struck by lightning, they become instantly petrified and fall to the ground where their body shatters upon impact.

A. Spiderwick

Ecclesiahabitans despuens
SPITTING GARGOYLE
RENDERED ONE-FOURTH ACTUAL SIZE

Gargoyles
FAMILY: BESTIALAPIDAE

Possibly a species of pygmy domesticated dragon, *gargoyles* actually cannot fly but are extremely agile and able to leap great distances, which may give them the illusion of flight. In fact, their movement is very similar to a monkey swinging through a jungle canopy. While not aquatic in makeup, they are efficient and excellent swimmers.

Only active at night, the gargoyle has adapted itself to remaining still for long periods of time so as to better guard the buildings on which it perches. With a stony skin that mimics brick and plaster, gargoyles are not affixed to building tops, but grip hold of them with incredible strength. Even though there may appear to be many gargoyles on a rooftop, only one will be a living creature.

They always look for the highest roosts possible, usually on cathedrals, skyscrapers, or other tall buildings.

~109~

This is a greater gargoyle I spotted on a trip to Cologne, Germany—it was a massive beast that lived up on one of the largest cathedrals I have ever seen.

PLATE XXXV

Perching stance

This small, feisty gargoyle was living on an old building in New York which is now a bank.

Small, webbed hands resemble wings but are incapable of flight.

Legs and feet are heavily muscled on this specimen.

It snorted quite a bit and made a growling croak sound.

Ecclesiahabitans nanus

DWARF GARGOYLE

RENDERED ONE-THIRD ACTUAL SIZE

PLATE XXXVI

Perching stance

This one was on a very old cathedral in Paris, France.

This particularly large creature had excellent vision and leaned far out from the edge of its perch to better observe what was happening down below it.

The skin was smooth, almost like marble, but it smelled like wet cement.

No tail on this one, despite its canine appearance.

A. Spiderwick

Ecclesiahabitans longicolleus
LONG-NECKED GARGOYLE
RENDERED ONE-SEVENTH ACTUAL SIZE

PLATE XXXVII

It appears that this one has two sets of ears and several simple eyes, like an insect.

Some reside in trees, others on the ground near well-traveled areas. This one was sighted in an old maple.

Phookas claim they can speak any language of man or animal.

The prehensile tail twitches when the phooka is annoyed, not unlike the tail of a cat.

A. Spiderwick

Praestigator fuscus
BLACK PHOOKA
RENDERED ONE-FOURTH ACTUAL SIZE

Like an owl, the phooka can rotate its head, but unlike an owl, the phooka rotates its head upside-down rather than front to back. This one claimed it gave him a better perspective.

Phookas
FAMILY: PRAESTIGIATORIDAE

This mischievous and roguish trickster can appear in the form of a horse, rabbit, goat, dog, or sometimes even a human. But no matter what form the *phooka* takes, its fur is almost always dark.

In horse form, a phooka will lure humans to ride on its back. Unlike the kelpie (see p. 52), however, the phooka will not do the rider any real harm but will take the unfortunate person on a wild and hair-raising ride.

On occasion the phooka can be persuaded to give advice and has been known to shepherd people away from great danger. For these reasons, despite the phooka's delight in confounding and terrifying humans, it is considered more benevolent than malevolent.

It is the phooka who spoils the blackberries after the first of November. Anyone who eats one after that date is stealing from the phooka and likely to be on the receiving end of this faerie's displeasure or devious sense of humor.

-113-

Some phookas prefer the shape of a small pony.

BLACKBERRIES (Rubus sp.) from a field where a talking horse was sighted grazing

PLATE XXXVIII

Candentisphaera floccata
WILL-O'-THE-WISPS
RENDERED ACTUAL SIZE

Like magnificent fireflies, the ethereal wisps are breathtaking to see on a moonlit night.

Will-o'-the-Wisps
FAMILY: FALSILUCIDAE

The luminous *will-o'-the-wisps* are spotted deep in forests, swamps, and other desolate places and appear as glowing orbs that move slowly over the landscape. These phantom lights are called by many different names and are even sometimes thought to be the prank of some malicious faerie. Elves particularly delight in using will-o'-the-wisps as a source of illumination and decoration for their revels.

Lost travelers spotting wisps often believe they are seeing an artificial light and head toward it, causing them to become even more lost. Many have died, lost and alone, or fallen prey to some more dangerous faerie. As with stray sod, it is unlikely that the wisps know that they cause so much havoc for mortals. Even if they did, however, there is little reason to think that they would change.

- Many times will-o'-the-wisps were depicted as devils or demons because of their association with the death of the hapless human who followed their lights. Because their preferred habitat is more remote and distanced from civilized settlements, they are rarely seen anymore.

Wisps were attracted to my gas lantern when I brought it to a remote marsh. (The lantern also attracted hordes of insects, including biting flies and mosquitos.)

October 11th, 1916

Fanciful depiction of a will-o'-the-wisp copied from a woodcut, supporting the notion that some malevolent form was behind the glowing lights.

September 6th, 1935

I have received yet another letter of rejection from yet another scientific journal. I have come to dread the mail and to dread my wife's false sympathy. I know she is secretly pleased that the larger world agrees with her assessment of my life's work. It is worthless. She tells me that perhaps I would be better suited writing for children and that I should make up faerie stories for our little daughter, but what she means is that I should give up science entirely.

Ironically, the fey have become increasingly agitated as the Guide nears completion. It may be best for me to hide it away where it cannot be stolen. I meet with the elder elves tonight. I fear that they are going to issue some kind of ultimatum.

Arthur Spiderwick disappeared in September of 1935, leaving his wife, Constance, and his young daughter, Lucinda, behind. Constance died soon afterward and Lucinda was sent to live with relatives, leaving the Spiderwick estate abandoned.

The Spiderwick estate was boarded up for many years, and, although Lucinda tried to take possession of it after she came of age, the many faerie attacks she endured led to her being institutionalized. The house remained uninhabited by humans until Jared, Simon, and Mallory arrived with their mother, Helen. Upon the Guide being rediscovered, many faeries vied for possession of the tome. Happily, Arthur's goal of publication has finally been achieved now that this field guide has been made available to the public. In the interest of being thorough, Jared added some notes and corrections to Arthur's research that he felt were worth mentioning.

Dear Mrs. Black and Mr. DiTerlizzi:

I know that a lot of people don't believe in faeries, but I do and I think that you do too. After I read your books, I told my brothers about you and we decided to write. We know about real faeries. In fact, we know a lot about them.

The page attached to this one is a photocopy from an old book we found in our attic. It isn't a great copy because we had some trouble with the copier. The book tells people how to identify faeries and how to protect themselves. Can you please give this book to your publisher? If you can, please put a letter in this envelope and give it back to the store. We will find a way to send the book. The normal mail is too dangerous.

We just want people to know about this. The stuff that has happened to us could happen to anyone.

Sincerely,

Mallory, Jared, and Simon Grace

Addendum by Jared G.

page 6: A boggart can be changed back to a brownie if you are nice to it.

page 10: Ogres can also make themselves look like humans and really cause a lot of trouble!

page 19: Baby dragons do look like salamanders, but they are larger and not as colorful.

page 21: Turning your shirt inside out really does work on these critters.

page 31: if you are good to elves, they may grant a wish.

page 81: Goblins can move very fast, so be careful!

page 85: Dont trust hobgoblins! But their spit will give you the Sight for a little while.

page 88: Mulgarath was bad news, but we took care of him.

page 92: Full-grown dragons are smaller than Arthur thought, and they can jump really high.

J.G.

Thimbletack

Spit

Hogsqueel

J.G.

A Goblin

J.G.

FOR FURTHER READING

Arthur Spiderwick's research seems to be consistent with many fables and folklore from all over the world. If you want to learn more about faerie folk and other fantastical creatures, here are some titles we recommend.

Afanas'ev, Aleksandr, coll. *Russian Fairy Tales.* Translated by Norbert Guterman. New York: Pantheon Books, 1945.

Arrowsmith, Nancy, and George Moorse. *A Field Guide to the Little People.* New York: Hill and Wang, 1977.

Bett, Henry. *English Myths & Legends.* New York: Dorset Press, 1991.

Booss, Claire, ed. *Scandinavian Folk & Fairy Tales.* New York: Avenel Books, 1984.

Bord, Janet. *Fairies: Real Encounters with Little People.* New York: Carrol and Graf, 1997.

Bourke, Angela. *The Burning of Bridget Cleary.* New York: Viking, 2000.

Briggs, Katharine. *An Encyclopedia of Fairies: Hobgoblins, Brownies, Bogies and Other Supernatural Creatures.* New York: Pantheon Books, 1976.

_____. *The Vanishing People: Fairy Lore and Legends.* New York: Pantheon Books, 1978.

Douglas, Sir George, ed. *Scottish Folk & Fairy Tales.* London: Walter Scott, 1892. Reprint, Bath, England: Lomond Books, 2003.

Dragons. The Enchanted World Series. Amsterdam: Time Life Books, 1985.

Dwarfs. The Enchanted World Series. Amsterdam: Time Life Books, 1985.

Evans-Wentz, W. Y. *The Fairy-faith in Celtic Countries.* Oxford: Oxford University Press, 1911. Reprint, London: Colin Smythe, 1977.

Fairies and Elves. The Enchanted World Series. Amsterdam: Time Life Books, 1985.

Giblin, James Cross. *The Truth About Unicorns.* New York: HarperCollins, 1991.

Gregory, Lady Augusta. *Irish Myths and Legends.* Philadelphia: Running Press, 1998. Originally published as *Gods and Fighting Men: The True Story of the Tuatha de Danaan and of the Fianna of Ireland, Arranged and Put into English by Lady Gregory* (London: John Murray, 1910).

Hoff, Joan, and Marian Yeates. *The Cooper's Wife Is Missing: The Trials of Bridget Cleary.* New York: Basic Books, 2000.

Ingulstad, Frid, and Svein Solem. *Troll: The Norwegian Troll, Its Terrifying Life and History.* Translated by Joan Felicia Hendriksen. Oslo: Glydendal Norsk Forlag, 1993.

Keightley, Thomas. *The World Guide to Gnomes, Fairies, Elves, and Other Little People: A Compendium of International Fairy Folklore.* New York: Gramercy Books, 1978. Originally published as *The Fairy Mythology* (London: G. Bell, 1878).

Kirk, Robert. *The Secret Commonwealth of Elves, Fauns, and Fairies.* London: David Nutt, 1893.

Mac Manus, Dermot. *The Middle Kingdom: The Faerie World of Ireland.* London: Max Parrish, 1959. Reprint, Buckinghamshire, England: Colin Smythe, 1973.

Magical Beasts. The Enchanted World Series. Amsterdam: Time Life Books, 1985.

Olenius, Elsa, coll. *Great Swedish Fairy Tales.* Translated by Holger Lundbergh. New York: Delacorte, 1973.

O'Neill, J. P. *The Great New England Sea Serpent: An Account of Unknown Creatures Sighted by Many Respectable Persons Between 1638 and the Present Day.* New Camden, ME: Down East Books, 1999.

Page, Michael. *Encyclopedia of Things That Never Were.* New York: Viking, 1987.

Parry-Jones, D. *Welsh Legends & Fairy Lore.* New York: Marboro Books, 1992.

Phillpotts, Beatrice. *The Faeryland Companion.* New York: Barnes & Noble, 1999.

Purkiss, Diane. *At the Bottom of the Garden: A Dark History of Fairies, Hobgoblins, and Other Troublesome Things.* New York: New York University Press, 2000.

Rose, Carol. *Giants, Monsters & Dragons.* New York: W. W. Norton, 2000.

———. *Spirits, Fairies, Gnomes and Goblins: An Encyclopedia of the Little People.* Santa Barbara, CA: ABC-CLIO, 1996.

Scott, Michael. *Irish Folk & Fairytale Omnibus.* Vols. 1-2. London: Sphere Books, 1983–84. Reprint, vol. 3, New York: Barnes & Noble, 1993.

Shepard, Odell. *The Lore of the Unicorn.* London: George Allen and Unwin, 1930. Reprint, New York: Avenell Books, 1982.

Tame, David. *Real Fairies: True Accounts of Meeting with Nature Spirits.* Berkshire, England: Capall Bann, 1999.

Tregarthen, Enys. *Pixie Folklore and Legends.* Collected by Elizabeth Yates. New York: Gramercy Books, 1996. Originally published as *Piskey Folk: A Book of Cornish Legends* (New York: John Day, 1940).

Water Spirits. The Enchanted World Series. Amsterdam: Time Life Books, 1985.

White, T. H. *The Book of Beasts: Being a Translation from a Latin Bestiary of the 12th Century.* New York: G. P. Putnam's Sons, 1954. Reprint, New York: Dover, 1984.

Wimberly, Lowry Charles. *Folklore in the English & Scottish Ballads.* Chicago: University of Chicago Press, 1928. Reprint, New York: Dover, 1965.

Yeats, W. B., ed. *Fairy & Folk Tales of the Irish Peasantry.* London: W. Scott, 1888.

Dedicated to the memory of Jim Henson, who showed us there were many worlds to visit; all we had to do was open our eyes.

—Tony & Holly

ACKNOWLEDGMENTS

Tony would like to thank:

My pop & my family, Ellen & Julie, Meno, Danya, Maddison,
Heidi & Jane, Joey B., Brian & Wendy (for the kind words,
and inspiring me), Kevin (you made my dreams come true *again*!),
Dan P., Rick, and the entire S&S team, and most of all Angela—
I couldn't have done this without your love and support.

Holly would like to thank:

Wayne Miller for the Latin translations, Heidi Stemple for her
help with folklore research, Kevin Lewis for his editorial guidance,
Theo Black for keeping me more or less sane, and Tony DiTerlizzi,
for the book that inspired everything.

SIMON & SCHUSTER BOOKS FOR YOUNG READERS · An imprint of Simon & Schuster Children's
Publishing Division · 1230 Avenue of the Americas, New York, New York 10020 · This book is a work of fiction. Any
references to historical events, real people, or real locales are used fictitiously. Other names, characters, places,
and incidents are products of the author's imagination, and any resemblance to actual events or locales or
persons, living or dead, is entirely coincidental. · Copyright © 2005 by Tony DiTerlizzi and Holly Black · All rights
reserved, including the right of reproduction in whole or in part in any form. · SIMON & SCHUSTER BOOKS FOR
YOUNG READERS is a trademark of Simon & Schuster, Inc. · Book design by Dan Potash · 10 9 8 7 6 5 4 3 2 1 · CIP
data for this book is available from the Library of Congress. · ISBN-13: 978-0-689-85941-0 · ISBN-10: 0-689-85941-4

Arthur Spiderwick's original handmade Guide was full of notes, observations, sketches, and watercolor studies of plates he was in the process of preparing for publication. Unfortunately, after years of improper storage much of the book was damaged and brittle, making an exact facsimile impossible to make.

Using Arthur's drawings and detailed descriptions, Tony painstakingly recreated many of Arthur's plates to the painted finish within this book. Holly researched Arthur's notations and corroborated them with existing folklore.

We reassembled the Guide in a more orderly fashion (by habitat) and produced the book as close as we could to the original, leaving in the old paper and the effects of time in an effort to uphold its authenticity.

Arthur Spiderwick (and Tony) primarily worked with gouache and pencil on bristol board. Arthur's handwriting was a bit hard to read, so in order to make it more legible, we typeset it in Emily Austin. His hand-titles were set in Preclusion. As with many old scientific books, we set the body text in Boswell.

The original field guide is in the possession of the Grace family at the Spiderwick estate.

In a man's torso
you will find

My secret
to all mankind

If false and true
can be the same

You will soon know
of my fame

Up and up and up
again

Good luck dear friend

LADDER TRUCK.

ment.

from
et

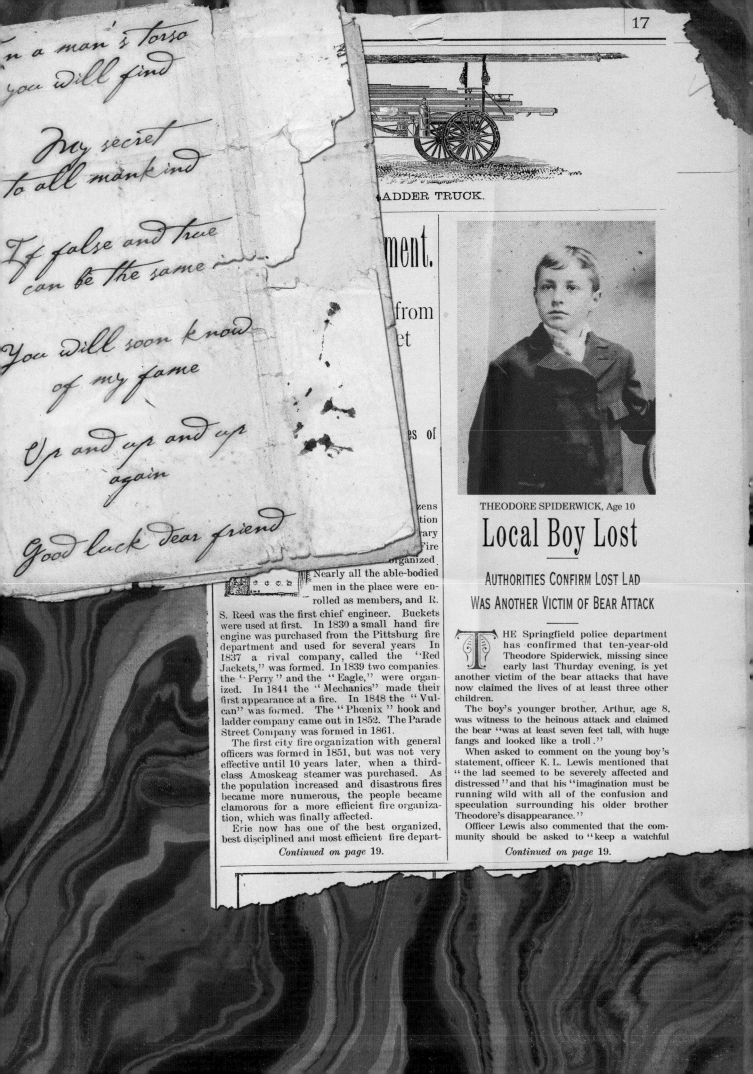

THEODORE SPIDERWICK, Age 10

Local Boy Lost

AUTHORITIES CONFIRM LOST LAD
WAS ANOTHER VICTIM OF BEAR ATTACK

zens
tion
rary
Fire
organized.
Nearly all the able-bodied men in the place were enrolled as members, and R. S. Reed was the first chief engineer. Buckets were used at first. In 1830 a small hand fire engine was purchased from the Pittsburg fire department and used for several years In 1837 a rival company, called the "Red Jackets," was formed. In 1839 two companies. the "Perry" and the "Eagle," were organized. In 1844 the "Mechanics" made their first appearance at a fire. In 1848 the "Vulcan" was formed. The "Phœnix" hook and ladder company came out in 1852. The Parade Street Company was formed in 1861.

The first city fire organization with general officers was formed in 1851, but was not very effective until 10 years later, when a third-class Amoskeag steamer was purchased. As the population increased and disastrous fires became more numerous, the people became clamorous for a more efficient fire organization, which was finally affected. Erie now has one of the best organized, best disciplined and most efficient fire depart-

Continued on page 19.

THE Springfield police department has confirmed that ten-year-old Theodore Spiderwick, missing since early last Thurday evening, is yet another victim of the bear attacks that have now claimed the lives of at least three other children.

The boy's younger brother, Arthur, age 8, was witness to the heinous attack and claimed the bear "was at least seven feet tall, with huge fangs and looked like a troll ."

When asked to comment on the young boy's statement, officer K. L. Lewis mentioned that "the lad seemed to be severely affected and distressed "and that his "imagination must be running wild with all of the confusion and speculation surrounding his older brother Theodore's disappearance."

Officer Lewis also commented that the community should be asked to "keep a watchful

Continued on page 19.